DINNER
AT THE
HAPPY
SKELETON

DINNER AT THE HAPPY SKELETON

◉ ◉ ◉

Chris Chalmers

J. Mendel Books

With thanks to Rolf for his encouragement, and Dave for giving me the wherewithal.

This book is for my godchildren, Ben and Emily.
(Just not yet.)

CHAPTER ONE

I love waking up next to Jack. He is five foot five, comedy small, so not what you'd call any of my types. But his skin is naturally smooth as a baby's; a bonus in a man of thirty-four. I nuzzle his head under my chin and try not to think of the spider-legs running amok over my own shoulders.

The red lights on his ceiling say 07:18. Another seven minutes till we are officially behind schedule.

'I need a slash,' he growls, in a voice cracked by dawn.

'Do Thunderbird Four,' I say. 'If you loved me you would ...'

Jack is cute, with chipmunk eyes and cheeks you want to bite. He is a living Action Man: compact and perfectly proportioned, with hair like a tennis ball. But he doesn't love me really.

Thank God.

He tuts as his head disappears. The hummock under the duvet shifts and deflates until his feet appear at the bottom of the bed. The rest of him follows as he folds into a heap on the carpet and crawls for the door ... It lacks the smooth entry and splosh of the little yellow submarine exiting the belly of Thunderbird Two. But it makes me laugh, every time.

At that moment there's a clink of china and a swish of designer silk as the bedroom door opens, narrowly missing Jack's head.

'Brew,' says Phil, stepping over him.

He puts three mugs on the bedside table. Then he slips out of his dressing gown and climbs back into the bed.

*

A threesome isn't something you go looking for. No, scratch that – it's exactly what you go looking for when you've been around the block as many times as I have. You just don't expect it to turn into anything.

I met Jack and Phil online the previous August. We chatted, suggestively, two or three times. I enjoyed the frisson of not knowing which of the two guys in the photos I was talking to; and since for once they were both quite tasty, it didn't matter.

As for the day we met – well, it was all quite Cynthia Payne …

So I'm sweaty and hungover, eager for fun if knackered from the night before, as I trudge up Denmark Hill with a rucksack full of sex toys. It takes me a while to find the address in a neat and tidy street that feels (no pun intended) anally suburban. Multi-hued children on tricycles clatter over paving stones, and though the net curtains aren't actually twitching like flamenco skirts, it feels like they should.

The taller one answers the door and shows me into the kitchen, where the shorter one is emptying the dishwasher from Sunday lunch. A tiny telly plays on the granite worktop as I tear a can of Fosters from the four-pack I picked up at Sainsbury's.

'I didn't know what to bring,' I say, rucksack betraying otherwise as it thuds on the terracotta flags.

Taller One slips the rest of the beers into the fridge.

The other, Jack, smiles and asks if I went out last night.

You have to watch out for that one, particularly when proceedings are at a delicate stage. On the London gay scene three years into a new millennium, you reveal your true colours by the club you patronise on a Saturday night: disco dolly, E-head, sleazeball, indie kid …

I opt for the most neutral of neutral opening gambits.

'Stayed in, actually. On click4dick.'

Jack nods approvingly, pouring himself a glass of wine.

'We went to Stirrups.'

The lightness of his tone makes it sound like a pony club, not the dark cutting edge of the London fetish scene. Then I notice the two pairs of rubber chaps outside on the washing line: one small, one medium, creaking on the breeze like the shed skins of superheroes.

Phil reappears, lighting a cigarette. I take him in properly for the first time: he is slim and gingery blond with stiletto shaped sideburns. Great skin too, though not for long judging by the way he's dragging on that ciggy. Like Jack, he is dressed in cool Sunday slobwear: trackie bottoms and a Calvin Klein tee.

'You all reet with that, Dan?' he asks, nodding at my beer, 'Cos I'm putting a brew on, like …'

He's a Geordie by the sound of it. An affable lot, I've always thought; warm and always up for fun. As presumably I'm about to find out.

*

We're still bantering in the kitchen as the TV peals out the theme to *Songs of Praise*. The three of us are connecting like old buddies who ran into each other by chance. We like the same old *French and Saunders* sketches and a lot of the same records. Jack and Phil laugh at all my best jokes; what more could you ask for?

Well, treacle tart. And interestingly, I get that too.

There it is, sitting in the fridge like a plateful of sticky sunshine as I pull out another beer. Phil made it for lunch, though between them they've shifted a churlishly small chunk. Treacle tart, you see, is My Very Favourite Thing, and never more than when post-alcohol sugar depletion has me craving a bit of pre-coital fortification. Some guys do drugs; I do treacle tart, and this one is Class A.

Two slices and another beer later, I'm uncommonly up for it as we skip up the stairs, which are carpeted in the sort of industrial-grade hessian favoured by interiors magazines. It helps that both guys are undeniably sexy – and that, despite a year's concerted online trawling, this is the first threesome I've ever pulled.

The sex, when we get to it, is highly acceptable. But just – you know, sex; albeit with one more of everything than I'm used to. Afterwards, I'm lying in the bed with Jack, basking in my own good fortune and a congealment that is two-thirds other people's. Phil is downstairs making tea. It turns out Phil makes a lot of tea, because he's only allowed to light up in the kitchen.

'We've had a chat,' says Jack from my armpit. 'And we were wondering if you'd like to meet up again.' He gives me this coaxing little smile which I'm soon to learn always gets its way.

'When did you do that?' I ask. They've hardly been out of my sight.

'When you were in the bathroom.'

We hadn't got going by that point, so this is a thumbs-up if ever there was one. Later, as I'm packing away my accoutrements, we schedule a rematch for the following weekend.

Jack and Phil are very nice men: good-looking, sweet, interesting, intelligent – ideal boyfriend material in fact, as they've both already discovered. I liked them when I arrived and I liked them when I left, which is not always the case with people you meet online.

I'm getting the bus home with a grin on my face I can't shift. Partly because I'm wondering what the pony-tailed girl on the next seat would say if she could see inside my rucksack. And partly because the bag itself is heavier by half a treacle tart.

Shrink-wrapped for hygiene, obviously.

CHAPTER TWO

There's a funny thing about the Northern line. Only one, mind. No matter when I get on the tube, I make it into the office at the same time every morning. While I'm on the train, a faceful of free newspaper keeps my mind off the job and on something scurrilous or scary instead (today: soldiers in Baghdad hauling down a statue of Saddam Hussein and whacking it with their shoes). It's only when my bum hits the chair at 9.25 that I start thinking about work.

My contract says office hours at Chartwell Shanks Wilkes O'Malley are nine to five-thirty. But this is advertising and I'm a groovy creative, so rebellion's in my blood. In my case, that amounts to dressing as sloppily as I like and spending nice long lunches at the gym. I work in a team with Sandra; she's the art director to my copywriter. She dreams up the visuals and I supply the words: headline and supporting text, old puns or current puns – whatever is required. Today, like most mornings, Sandra's at her desk when I arrive, sucking latte from the hair ribbons cascading from her tumbleweed topknot.

'Mornin' Dan,' she says flatly, chucking her empty cardboard cup at the bin and missing. 'I didn't get you one cos we're out of sweeteners, and I know what a temple your body is …'

Cow. It was her turn.

She takes one of her favourite scandal sheets from her handbag and flicks to a spread on celebrity bikini belly rolls.

'So, how were The Boys last night? Worship up to its usual standard … ?'

When you've spent five days a week in a glass box with someone for nearly a decade, you don't have many secrets. Sandra is privy to all but the most visceral details of my personal life, chewing them over with vicarious delight. After eighteen years of marriage and three unruly children, me and medical documentaries on Channel Five serve much the same purpose.

'Mind your own business, Desert Puss,' I toss good-naturedly over my shoulder, en route to the kitchen.

By the time I've had my coffee, answered two emails, ordered a limited-edition Gary Numan CD from Japan and found the weekend weather forecast for Helsinki, I'm raring to go. Assuming I can find some work to do … Chartwell Shanks is going through a quiet patch. In the latest economic doldrums, marketing directors are clinging to their budgets like remoras to a whale shark. Since the Champagne Charlies of the Square Mile have all put their mobiles on divert, Chartwell Shanks, specialists in financial advertising, is feeling the pinch more than most. We haven't had a decent creative brief across our desk in weeks. I reckon it's looking ominous – though Sandra, who's usually not above reading the runes of doom in a misplaced Magic Marker, reckons we're safe till the end of the summer.

'Those Big Plus TV ads will keep the place ticking over,' she says. 'The board won't go swinging the axe just yet …'

Big Plus is an insurance brand. It's part of Crown National plc, the biggest, starchiest player in the underwriting market. It was a shock two years ago when

Chartwell Shanks won the account from a top agency, in the advertising equivalent of Accrington Stanley beating Man U in the FA Cup. It earned us a begrudging column inch in *Agency Age*, the venerable industry rag; minnows like us are meant to keep to our own side of the pond.

It's quarter to eleven and I'm on eBay, wondering what to bid for a genuine 1966 Rolykin Dalek (boxed). I know that's the time because Cranleigh Fosdyke's corduroy blazer just slid past the glass partition on its way to the next office. Cranleigh is old-school advertising – fifty-five if he's a day – and a comforting rejoinder to the age-old question Sandra and I often ponder: 'Where *do* all the old creatives go?'

That's the end of his good side. Cranleigh is a pretentious arse, who has talked his way onto every decent brief this agency's had since we came here. Anyone else in Cranleigh Fosdyke's oxblood brogues would have risen to creative-directorhood years ago; but the role, like his penchant for hair mousse, doesn't suit him. Cranleigh is happy to bask in the glowing embers of his lineage from advertising royalty; his grandfather was the F-word in Fosdyke & Partners, a big overpowering cheese of an agency till it was gobbled up by J. Walter Thompson in the 1970s in return for a sea of cash. Word is, Cranleigh has been turning down job offers for years, in favour of three cushy days a week as erudite wit, dropper of pearls and occasional writer of copy at Chartwell Shanks.

Needless to say, on the day when the sexy new TV brief for Big Plus finally emerges from Account Handling, it is he our esteemed boss, Lionel Shanks, calls into his office. Every creative in the place has been anticipating this moment for weeks; us included.

'Like waiting for a wolfhound to shit out your car keys,' is Sandra's pithy assessment.

She has a point. By the time the brief plops onto Lionel's distressed Formica desk, a fortnight's creative pencil-chewing has already been lost. The suits have been hoarding the strategy like the last spliff at Woodstock. The only clue filtering down from Astrid Brazier, our head of Account Handling, is that the Big Plus brand message has 'undergone a *pur-retty* radical overhaul' since we put them on telly last year.

So when the proposition – the unique kernel of creative-drool-inducing insight – is finally revealed, Sandra and I know better than to be surprised. Quite how 'Big Plus works harder to give you more' is a seismic shift away from 'Big Plus goes further to give you better service' has us stumped.

'Fucking bag-carriers!' says Sandra, flipping through the brief she filched from Lionel's desk while he was on the fire escape with a Lucky Strike. 'We could've started weeks ago if we'd known all they were gonna do was play lucky-dip with the sore-arse!'

Ever since her Lewisham childhood, Sandra's specific form of dyslexia means she defaults to the nearest obscenity whenever she's stumped for a word. Hence 'sore-arse', her eye-watering approximation of Roget's lexicon.

As the hours and days tick away, it becomes obvious the coveted brief is never officially coming our way. This doesn't stop Sandra perking up like a meerkat every time Lionel passes our office, or arriving each morning with a new campaign scrawled on detritus from her handbag. And yet we know, it is Lionel and Cranleigh alone who are destined to see that shining beacon of righteousness – The Answer To The Brief. Till then, their musings are meant to be confidential, but Sandra's curiosity is insatiable. Which is why, three days before the client presentation, she is engaging Astrid in the ladies at the hand-dryer moment.

'How's it going on Big Plus?' she asks innocently.

Astrid's fingers pause mid-shuffle in a clink of white-gold bands.

'The guys are doing a fantastic job,' she says, checking her roots in the mirror. 'They've got right behind the strategy and, as an agency, we're all singing off the same hymn sheet. I couldn't be more delighted – *really*.'

Sandra leans into her reflection to fish for an imaginary contact lens. 'And is it true they're going with the Oompa-Loompas?'

We've both seen the TV storyboards knocking around the studio: Roald Dahl's friendly orange gremlins, coming to the rescue in your every insurance nightmare.

'Yup!' says Astrid. 'That's on the table, no two ways about it.' She knits her eyebrows, raising a finger like an aerial receiving signals from the mothership. 'It's got class. It's got empathy with the grey market, cos they all remember the original film … And the kids'll love it cos it's poking fun at dwarves!'

Sandra fiddles with one of many earrings; a stag beetle caught in amber. 'You do know they're shooting a remake of *Willy Wonka and the Chocolate Factory*, don't you, Astrid? With politically correct Oompa-Loompas?'

Our head of Account Handling admires her cheekbones in the mirror, pouting till it looks like she's trying to inhale her upper lip.

'No problem … That'll just give us retro chic.

Everyone will compare ours with the originals.'

Sandra, who wears jewellery the way a shipwreck wears barnacles, unthreads bangles off one wrist onto the other. 'And you do know the film producers have just done a big media tie-in? With Linlithgoe Holdings?'

The corporation that owns our client's biggest competitor.

Astrid freezes mid-moue and a hand flies to her breastbone. 'Where the hell did you hear that?'

'This week's *Agency Age*,' says Sandra sweetly. 'First page of the Media section, halfway down. There's a copy in—'

The door to the ladies bangs like a truck-stop hooker.

'Reception.'

CHAPTER THREE

Quickly, quietly, as a result of this conflict of interests, the Oompa-Loompas die in the night. Behind closed doors, creative director Lionel and star player Cranleigh set to with their layout pads. They are men on a mission, hell-bent on whelping an ad campaign to rock the financial services industry on its sensible heels. Sometimes they leave the office altogether, for the contemplative nirvana of the bar at the Carriage House Hotel. Once they're off-site, even Lalita, Lionel's pint-sized Filipina P.A., is forbidden to trouble their mobiles.

Sandra and I still aren't in on the brief, but we can't resist one last tilt. The tricky bit is getting our work under Lionel's nose, which Sandra achieves with dogged aplomb: at the photocopier, as he's unpicking a paper jam; outside the second-floor gents; and once, in passing, at the bagel stall in Victoria Station. Every time Lionel thanks her, promising to take a look when he gets a minute; then he asks how we're doing with our half-column, black-and-white, type-only trade ad for Dromgoole Equitable's Yen Hedged Multi-Level Bond Fund ... As he's quick to point out, 'It's a great opportunity!'

With a day to go, the account handlers are getting fractious. Astrid has a one-to-one meeting with Lionel in his office. She stands for the full two hours, occasionally leaning a Laura Ashley-print shoulder on the glass partition. She wields a wad of typed A4 that she slaps on the table to make her point as she speaks. Lionel says little; just nods sagely at intervals, thrusting out his lower lip like a faulty cash till.

At 3 p.m. that afternoon, the buzz goes round the agency: *Lionel and Cranleigh have cracked it!*

'Go on,' says Sandra, leaning tremulously over her PC, 'guess what they've come up with this time …'

For someone who changes all her passwords to 'BOLLUCKS' (sic) on the grounds that it pops into her head when she forgets it, Sandra has a knack for accessing other people's documents.

I mentally sift through Lionel and Cranleigh's favourite creative ideas. 'Um – something unoriginal that says problem/solution. Padlock-and-key, or a jigsaw puzzle?'

'No.'

'A pastiche of some arty Polish film no one's heard of but Lionel?'

'Uh-uh.'

'Then it has to be a straight-to-camera waffle, by that *Sunday Telegraph* columnist Cranleigh knows from yachting!'

That's all their usual fallbacks.

Sandra clasps her knees primly. 'Try one more for mummy …'

'Oh, I dunno – some typographical crap you can't read? Navy-blue lettering on a black background? Come on, tell me!'

'Close!' she grins. 'Look at these …'

I peer over her shoulder as she scrolls through the TV scripts. Each features an animated Big Plus symbol, coming to the rescue of burst pipes, missed planes and sickly pets, in a range of thirty-second scenarios. And each culminates in the weighty strapline: You're Minus the Hassle with Big Plus.

No two ways about it. Lionel and Cranleigh have done it again.

*

Somehow – don't ask me why – the client buys it.

Which means the rest of us are left holding the fort while Lionel, Cranleigh, Astrid and a springy young account exec who has caught her eye buckle down to the gruelling task of shooting the ads. This means a week in a nice little studio in Camden with full catering, then a location shoot in leafy English suburbia. Which, once the client is persuaded of the importance of guaranteed sunshine, is to be found ten miles outside Cape Town. That's followed by a further week of post-production, and a weekend at the Crown National chairman's country pile in Sussex for the campaign's champagne premiere to the company top brass.

Call me bitter, but I'd give a hardback first edition of *Doctor Who and the Zarbi* to be in Lionel's and Cranleigh's shoes as they bask in all that crucial South African sunshine. (Why wouldn't I? I've got three copies.) As it is, Sandra and I have no excuse but to be our own bosses, which entails taking even longer lunches at the gym as our workload drifts down to zero.

All of which means, when the inevitable happens, it feels like the plot of a faintly familiar movie. Advertising is a rollercoaster business at the best of times. So I know what's coming, from the moment Lalita's glossy crimped head whips round the door and says, 'Dan – Lionel says can you pop through?'

*

Inside his office, the air-con sucks gamely at forbidden fag smoke.

The creative director is standing by the round meeting table, eyes downcast. Lionel Shanks is a fashion victim, who distracts from the meagre hand fate dealt him in the looks department with couture polo necks. He favours photochromic specs by Ace of Shades, which have the effect of wearing him.

'Sit down, Dan,' he says.

Even on a good day, Lionel has the air of an undertaker who just called in the receivers, and right now I'm getting it in spades. As I take my place at the table, I notice a bottle of water and three tumblers (three! I see where this is going ...) He's still standing, staring at the floor like Leonard Cohen consulting a particularly melancholy set list. The silence is killing me; I'm tempted to inject a bit of levity by saying grace, but abruptly he speaks.

'As you know, Dan, the agency's going through a tough time. Revenues have taken a dive, and the only thing keeping us afloat is the TV work for Big Plus.'

I check him for signs of smugness. There are none.

'Alas, Crown National are losing money hand over fist. I took a phone call from the chairman last night. He's ordered us to pull the entire campaign with immediate effect.'

That little bombshell explains his lack of smugness. Bless him, Lionel's eyes are watering. It's all I can do to stop myself squeezing his shoulder; we both know what's coming, and so far it's hurting him more than me.

'As a consequence, the Chartwell Shanks board met this morning, and took the regrettable decision that redundancies must be made.'

There it is: the Big R!

That means a cheque; it could be a nice one! (Come on, Lionel – let the dog see the rabbit!)

'Dan, I am legally obliged to inform you that you, among others, are being considered for redundancy. I strongly advise you to consult a solicitor.'

Blimey, steady on – this is getting heavy.

'Have I done something wrong, Lionel?'

At last he looks me in the eye.

'No, you haven't. But there are procedures we have to follow, for your protection as well as ours.'

He gathers himself by pouring water into two glasses. He's taking care to get the words just right.

'According to the terms of your contract, you will be salaried for the duration of your notice period, though you are not required to come into work after today …'

Wow: immediate holiday! Shit: I'm unemployed!

'… We will also be making financial compensation over and above your legal entitlement, in recognition of the upheaval this will cause.'

Nice one, Lionel! How much would that be, then? A week for every year of service? A month? How many M&S Steam Cuisines will it buy before I have to pound the streets with my portfolio?

He's read my mind. 'I can't give you an exact figure, but if you see Denzil after this meeting he'll give you the bottom line.'

Now there's an offer. Denzil Wilkes is the agency's finance director, who I quite fancy in a Fertile-Dad-at-Debenhams sort of way. Not exactly a rippling Adonis, but in Chartwell Shanks' limited firmament of eye candy, he's a Star Bar among cough drops.

'Sorry, Dan, but that's that,' says Lionel quietly. He looks like he needs a drink, though he hasn't touched his glass. 'Any questions?'

A car boot sale of emotions clutter my head. I am horrified, relieved, elated and subdued all at once. I'll think of a hundred things the moment I walk out of the door, but right now I can't think of one.

I shake my head and take a sip of water. My eyes come to rest on the last empty glass.

'Shall I, er … ?'

'Send Sandra through!'

CHAPTER FOUR

We both know what will happen if we go to the pub.

Unlike most the creatives at Chartwell Shanks, Sandra and I aren't big daytime drinkers. Even in ordinary circumstances, more than a glass of wine for her and two pints of pissy lager for me sees us slouched and useless for the rest of the afternoon; fit for nothing but surfing the net for thrills (me) and glassy-eyed rambling to the HRT helpline (her). But today is different. With no desks to go back to, no thumbnail-sized proofs from the studio panting for our sign-off, we'd get absolutely legless, albeit for different reasons.

In the office, we're a twosome: *Sandrandan / Danansandra* – a single, seamless being. Outside, our lives couldn't be more different. She's got three kids to feed; I've got a DVD collection. She has four rambling Victorian storeys with a dodgy roof in Kilburn; I've got one-and-a-half beds in Clapham. Her salary is eaten up in school fees, outgrown trainers and airfares times five; I fritter away mine on dusty sci-fi toys and weekend breaks anywhere I fancy.

The sun is shining as we walk to Victoria Station. We're both in shock, but at different points on the spectrum. We've seen Denzil, separately, who went through the figures like someone just died. It's all meant to be Secret Squirrel, though judging by the doe-eyed looks and eggshell paces we encountered as we left the office, the word is out.

'Dave'll go spare,' says Sandra as we go through the ticket barrier to the Underground. Her husband is paranoid about money at the best of times. 'Beans on toast in the kitchen tomorrow – you'll see!'

The next day is their wedding anniversary. They had a table booked at the Kensington Grill till she called Dave with the news. He's cancelled it.

At the bottom of the escalator I'm still in a daze as she pecks me on the cheek.

'See you at the solicitors …'

I give her a hug and tell her not to let Dave grind her down. Sandra and I have worked and played, rowed and nearly wet ourselves laughing every day since her youngest was in nappies. He starts secondary school in September. I think she's amazing, the way she keeps kids, career and home all spinning on canes, but I'm not sure I've ever told her. Working with someone is like that.

Just then, a knot of pensioners with tartan wheelie suitcases steam past, almost knocking us sideways. I never use the tube at two in the afternoon and can't believe how busy it is. But then I'm not exactly in a hurry, am I?

'Sod this, Sand,' I yell, waving her goodbye down the entrance to the Victoria line. 'I'm going to yomp!'

*

You get a skewed idea of distances when you do most of your travelling thirty metres underground. Me and driving never got on, so I bought a flat by a tube station instead. But being spared the one-way systems and the endless quests for unclampable parking, means that, even after nearly twenty years, I've never grasped how London's neighbourhoods fit together.

That partly changed the day a tube strike coincided with a fire at our local bus garage, and I had no choice but to walk to work. Turned out I could cover the distance from my flat to the office in just under an hour. A quick scan of the *A–Z* lopped off five minutes more. And, while it doesn't rival that guy who crossed America via other people's swimming pools, the route is mostly park, river, bijou shops and the perimeter fence of Chelsea Barracks' parade ground: in other words, pretty scenic all the way.

When the weather's good, I've been known to yomp to work two or three times a week if I'm not staying over with The Boys. It feels green and rather responsible, and you can't knock the extra cardiovascular. Sometimes I'll yomp home again too – and on days like this when I can't face the tube, it's a welcome escape.

Over the river, I head through the gates into Battersea Park. The sun is shining, the borders are blooming; it's a Thursday afternoon at the end of April, and I don't have a reason in the world not to follow my nose. I take a detour to the riverside walk; watch the grey water of the Thames swill against the bank ... Funny – everything was normal when I woke up this morning. Now it's upside down. The last time this happened, I was in my first job in advertising. Back then, redundancy threw me into a blind panic – though it did bring a cheque for three grand, which was the biggest I'd ever seen with my name on it. Thirteen years on, that cheque is going to be appreciably bigger. Not a fortune; not by City Boy standards, and not if you've got three kids and a neurotic husband to feed. But with my last month's salary on top, a little under fifteen grand ain't bad at all. There's lawyers to see first, of course. Papers to sign and hands to shake. But that's the upshot: *fifteen-beautiful-K!*

Far above the river a heron comes in to land on the highest branches of a plane tree. It stands for a moment on the rustling circumference, then folds into a sitting position as its mate emerges from the foliage beside it. The second one takes off in a papery swoop, swinging away downriver ... Here's me with all the time in the world, while up there, in the nesting zone, they're clocking on, clocking off.

The park is quiet. Criminally so in the sunshine. The kids are at school and the suckers are at work, so it's just me, the mums and the pushchairs. Except they're not all mums. They're easy enough to spot: sulky mouth, Crazy Colour hair and a papoose dressed better than she is means 'she' is the au pair.

I buy an ice cream and find a bench in the sun. One pound sixty for a Mr Whippy with sprinkles! Need to watch that, for a start: chuck my money around, and it'll be gone in no time ...

I pull a calculator from my bag and start tapping. As dreamy Denzil explained, a redundancy payoff is tax-free, so what you see is what you get. Which means, when the money comes through, I'm looking at near-as-dammit five months' salary! So allowing, say, a month to find some work, and another before I get paid once I've found it – that means I can safely take three months off.

Three months!
Off!

Thirteen weeks; ninety-odd days. I call that the best part of a summer, all for me. I've only had more than a fortnight off three times since I started working – Australia, New Zealand and hepatitis. With the first two, three weeks seemed like an aeon; a Fabergé egg of a holiday, shamelessly and exquisitely luxurious. Now I could put all three of them together, minus the jaundiced eyeballs and bed rest, and still have four weeks on top! I can barely comprehend it.

Anyway, that's one option. I finish my ice cream and stroll across the park, skirting the edge of the lake. I don't have to take a break at all, do I? The way work's been the last couple of months, I'm hardly in need of a holiday, and it's not long since I had a week in the Canaries.

I could look for a job straight away. Chances are it'll take a while, but when I do find one, I'm quids in. Ten, twelve grand maybe – just like that. I could whop it into the mortgage, cut years off the repayments like I'm always telling punters to do in my tedious ads for Parapet Mortgages.

I'm feeding the stub of the ice-cream cone to an appreciative mallard when I see a kite. It's sailing high on strings above the trees; a red and yellow giant, swooping geometrically against the graph-paper blue of the sky. The flier, a hefty lad with his shirt off, is fighting to keep control. He tenses himself against the strain, as the kite bounces off invisible walls like a housefly in a holding pattern. By the time I reach the gate I must have looked over my shoulder a dozen times. Who'd have thought a man's back, shining in the sun like that, could be so aesthetically engaging …

At Battersea Park Station, the first bedraggled

drones of the evening are scurrying home for a few hours' grace. In the morning they'll retrace these steps, begrudging but clean and briefly creaseless.

'*Mortgage, my arse!*' I tell a Lycra-clad cycle courier.

I don't actually mean to say it out loud – but he sweeps by anyway, oblivious.

CHAPTER FIVE

I wonder what Maxine Prince would say if she knew three men were sleeping in her bed tonight. According to Phil's contact on the front desk, the R&B diva was staying in our suite last week, on the solitary Finnish date of her world tour. Whatever she thought, I've no doubt the Grand Union Hotel, Helsinki, is a bigger revelation to me than it was to her. I'm new to five-star.

Don't get me wrong, I've been around. I did the math, and Finland makes it thirty-eight countries, which is nearly one for every year of my life – but only ever economy standard. As a rule, when I go away I go to see somewhere new, experience something different. Carpet plushness and the shagginess of the bath towels have never been a priority. But thanks to The Boys, I've crashed the glass ceiling into five-star – and it didn't hurt a bit.

Jack and Phil both work in the City, and they're attuned to the finer things in life. You can see it in their luggage, standing at the gilded door where the big blond bellhop left it. Two complementary Louis Vuittons versus my hardy rucksack. The Boys like their designer labels, especially Phil. Wherever we've been – Prague, Florence, Madrid – he's exercised his talent for tracking down the equivalent of Bond Street in the time it takes me to unfold the map.

A card clicks in the door slot. The electrics chirp and in they come.

'Sound!' says Phil with a glint of satisfaction. 'Sonja-

Kristina's booked us the à la carte restaurant for tonight. On the house, like!'

He takes off his jacket and puts it on a hanger. Jack starts unpacking, toiletries first. The Boys have their sweet little symbioses, and this is one of them: Phil packs, Jack unpacks. I shield myself with a satin throw as a Clinique Under-Eye Moisturiser narrowly misses my head.

'Shift your lazy arse,' says Jack with a smile, 'and make that filthy rucksack disappear before it rots the carpet!'

I slide off the big bed and unzip my bag. Our suite offers a choice of wardrobes, both slightly smaller than my bathroom at home. Inside, hangers shine like new coins and the shelves are lined with scented paper. A white bathrobe hangs in each, monogrammed with the hotel crest. There's a third robe folded on the single bed. Whenever we go away, there's always another bed in situ. Phil gives the duvet a cursory ruffle every morning, so as not to scandalize the chambermaid.

My clothes are stowed; my diary and my *Doctor Who* magazine are on the bedside table. In five minutes, I'm done.

'No porn!' announces Phil, tossing the remote onto a Queen Anne chair.

'You're *kwidding*!' comes a toothbrush-hampered voice from the bathroom. Jack likes his porn.

'Come on,' I say, 'let's go down and have a drink.'

I'm having a pee before we hit the bar when I spot The Boys' tubes and bottles, lined up against the brushed-chrome splashback like an early Damien Hirst. Not even R&B divas travel with this many toiletries, I think, as the toilet flushes with a respectful hum.

Of course, it's always possible Maxine Prince would be delighted to know there are three blokes in her bed tonight. If you believe what you read on the net, she's that kind of girl.

*

We've had this Helsinki trip arranged for ages: a cosmopolitan-sounding jaunt to somewhere none of us has ever been. Like most of our trips, we're here from Thursday evening to Sunday afternoon. That way, we get two full days plus whatever excitement Friday and Saturday night have to offer – all for a single precious day of annual leave, which is vital. Or, in my case, it used to be.

We have no plans for the weekend beyond our usual whistle-stop tour of the essential sites and fleshpots. Thursday night is drinks and dinner. I resist the urge to cause a fracas in the hotel restaurant, because we've a wealthy, well-connected mate of Phil's to thank for the very reasonable rate we're paying. But, sophisticated as he thinks he is, even Phil baulks at bear on the menu. The new chef is Russian; I make a mental note to miss breakfast.

Friday passes swimmingly enough. A museum here, a gallery there. Then a photo opportunity at a funky monument to the composer Sibelius who, judging by the bust, was a dead ringer for Basil Fawlty. To the passers-by of Helsinki we look like three guys-about-town, with nothing to imply there's more to our arrangement than meets the eye. I mean, it's not as if we skip around hand-in-hand like Bananarama.

Gay men are keen on threesomes. I daresay plenty of

straight people are too, or would be if they could arrange them as easily as your metropolitan homosexual. In terms of recreational sex, some single guys seek them out in preference to one-on-ones. They develop an aptitude for them, and it's quite an art. To be adept at pulling threesomes, you need to be like the top-selling brand of dog food: irresistibly appealing to a range of different consumers.

Threesomes fall into two categories: 2 + 1, and 1 + 1 + 1. The first is easier to arrange, since it only involves one set of negotiations. In a lifetime of attempted debauchery, it is the only kind that's come my way. They are particularly popular with couples in long-term relationships, because the longer it is, the more chance they'll need a boost in the bedroom department. And the more chance the relationship will stand it.

Jack and Phil have been together six years and lived together for five. The decision to add a side order to their carnal menu was recent and carefully considered. Neither of them, they said, wanted to cheat on the other. At the same time, they'd reached the conclusion that the only thing hornier than a bloke is two blokes, so something had to give. That's when they started surfing the net and frequenting places like Stirrups.

Gay London boasts half a dozen clubs where drink, drugs and dancing defer to sex as the prime raison d'être. You telegraph your availability simply by being there, plainly as walking round with a butt plug behind your ear. Etiquette differs from man to man. Some go in for the on-site grapple, while others prefer to carry the spoils back to their lair. The Boys are full of tales from their nights on the wild side, and I've insisted on hearing them all. They range from encounters of enviable passion with silken skinheads, to a memorable liaison with a plasterer who sleepwalked into their spare room and pissed all over their free weights. Their most successful conquests make it into their mobile phone directory, for a potential repeat engagement. But reconstituted meat, they have found, is rarely a match for the fresh stuff – and in London, fresh meat is always in season. So the fact that our own Sunday afternoon curtain-twitcher became a regular thing is a surprise to us all. Not least because it turned out to be about more than just sex.

Like fun, for instance. And looking out for each other. And, in their case, acting as a sounding board for my insecurities – not least my recent career blip. After the initial euphoria, being made redundant has dented my ego. It's hijacked my sense of fun a bit too, though I'm trying to keep that to myself. The Boys work hard and they deserve a weekend off from tending my wounded pride. On top of that, it isn't just me who's out of sorts. I've twice caught Phil wearing that expression that says 'Tread carefully'.

Phil is like two-way plush. Soft to the touch, but when you rub him the wrong way you expose his darker side. And since I have him to thank for the ridiculously low rate I'm paying for three nights in taffeta-swag heaven, it is wise to proceed with caution.

*

Following our usual pattern, if Friday is culture then Saturday is shopping. Or what there is of it. The Helsinki equivalent of Oxford Street feels more like Balham High Road with smarter raincoats. And where central London has a dozen department stores, Helsinki has Stockmann: a tidy operation on five floors selling everything from a pin to a bear trap.

I used to like clothes shopping alone, but it's something else I've found can be fun in threes. The Boys are patient, honest in their opinions, and we pretty much agree on what looks good. Style-wise, Jack and I favour mainstream casual with a soupçon of gay-boy chic. Phil is more flamboyant. He drools over glossy fashion mags, can see the merit in asymmetrical cuffs and uncomfortable-looking ruching. He longs for couture labels, although Jack, holder of the purse strings, rarely lets him indulge in more than the sanitised, high-street version. That doesn't stop him fondling sleeves and trying on; Phil can sweep out of the changing room in something by Versace that on the rail resembled an artistic response to head injuries – and look amazing. Colours, stripes and patterns all love him, and cameras do, too. In the photos from our previous trips, Phil never looks less than elegant. Jack, cute as he is, looks small and puffy-cheeked; I look like I've forgotten how to smile but I'm having a crack anyway.

Phil did acting in his teens. He was on the verge of a part in a movie when his stepdad duffed him up for getting too big for his Sunderland boots and burned his show reel in a skip. Battle lost and bottle gone, he gave it all up; or that's how he tells it. Phil lives in a world where everything is black or, alternatively, white. He's always at all-out war or perfect peace with everyone. There's no in-between, and it does make you wonder. Fond of him as I am, kind as he can be, I never completely trust him. And he knows it.

Jack, I do trust. He can see things from two sides. He's more cautious, like me, which makes him and Phil an odd combination. Our wacky triumvirate aside, I know I couldn't cope with Phil as a boyfriend. I'm not sure how Jack does, but he never complains. From where I'm standing they seem like a very happy couple.

Phil is sifting through a rail of Issey Miyake shirts when I pad out of the changing cubicle minus my shoes. It's not like I need another pair of khaki combat trousers but a bargain's a bargain, especially in euros.

'How do they look?' I ask.

Jack puts down the stack of black turtlenecks he's riffling through for an elusive small. He walks round me, appraising my backside then gives it a playful pinch.

'Very nice, fella. Colour matches your eyes.'

In which case, sold to the man in socks. My eyes are one of the few bits of my body I like.

'What do you reckon, Phil?' I ask diplomatically.

'Aye,' he says, sailing past with an armful of strategically crushed linen. 'They look reet enough.'

The cubicle snaps shut with an angry clatter of curtain rings.

Uh-oh ...

Fifteen minutes later, it's still light outside as we trundle through the carousel doors. Phil wants coffee, which means he needs a fag. He's tense, the way I've seen him before when he's about to blow. Jack knows how to handle him; he can divert the eruption when it comes and sometimes diffuse it altogether. I tend to make it worse, so I've learned the value of the tactical withdrawal. In two-and-a-bit hours, we're booked into a bear-free restaurant recommended by Phil's friend on reception. So while The Boys head across the street to a yummy-looking cake shop, I make an excuse about saving myself for dinner and say I'll see them later.

I feel in my pocket for the map I picked up at the hotel.

Time to go walkabout.

CHAPTER SIX

In the days of my childhood, whenever I found myself on an alien high street, there was one place I always had to find.

WHSmith. I don't know why.

It didn't matter that every branch looked and smelled the same; that was how it should be. I felt compelled to take a reassuring look at the mags, pens, records and, most of all, the books. How could I cross back through the intergalactic boundary of Preston, Chorley or Poulton-le-Fylde without checking the *Doctor Who* books were where they should be?

I grew up in small-town Lancashire. Till a solid if unspectacular English degree – and my parents' belief that I had more chance of a job if I moved to London – opened up the world in ways none of us expected. In the intervening years, the impulse to seek out WHSmiths has been replaced by a more cosmopolitan if just as irresistible tic. Nowadays, I can't leave a city with an Olympic stadium without taking a look.

To my mind, no architectural gem lifts a city like the hallowed home of the Olympiad. When I was a kid, the Games were as good as it got. A treat you ran home for, up there with the Daleks, the showjumping and Crufts. Everything about the Olympics was cool; anyone who'd ever taken part, a borderline deity. Like that waiter I met in Fort Lauderdale, he of the inevitable five-ring tattoo. Brad may have been girly and grungy, out of condition *and* the calamari special, but he'd skated for

Canada in Sarajevo and that was good enough for me.

Helsinki held the summer Games in 1952. Everything I know about them comes from a sticker album that came free with petrol when I was about ten. So I step off the tram a stop before the stadium, all the better for experiencing their legacy to the full. I'm in a very different part of the city, a land of parks and flyovers, far from any hint of metropolitan self-importance. As I pause at my third cast-iron horseman of the day a tram rattles by, leaving in its wake a view of the whitish walls of the stadium. I imagine these streets back in the day, ringing with twenty different languages as dignitaries strolled and gentlemen of the press ran to their marks with cumbersome cameras bouncing on their chests.

At the entrance there's no one around. Just a girl behind the desk who sells me a ticket in humiliatingly perfect English. The lift man rips it in half and pushes a button so we creak up to the top of the tower. Through the mesh of the observation deck, the city lights are coming on against the dusk. Beyond the stadium walls I see hockey pitches and what could be a swimming pool. Below is the running track, and the brownish turf where throwers and jumpers heaved about. But where once there were throwing circles, now there are goalposts. Sacrilege, but probably economic necessity. The spectator stands themselves look tiny, empty but for resting crows and a groundsman mending a seat. Yet, forlorn as it seems, there's still the essence of glory in the faded ley lines of those lane markings.

The groundsman packs up his tools, ready to head off for the night. It's chilly up here – not surprisingly. From the messy spirograph of the route map in the inflight magazine, I learned Helsinki is on a level with the Shetlands. The lights of the city grow more like dewdrops every minute, and I wish I'd brought my camera; not that the pictures would come out. I once took twenty shots of a full moon because the surface bore a Turin Shroud-like image of Margaret Thatcher. I thought it was an omen of her imminent death and I could flog them to the papers. It wasn't of course; the pictures were crap too.

I'm about to get back in the lift when the groundsman pauses at the main gate, where the heroic marathon class of '52 would have stumbled through for a final glorious circuit of the stadium.

Except, that's no athlete he is talking to through the bars. Far from it.

I know exactly who it is, even in the half-light, even at this distance. Even after eight years.

Some things about a person never change. Like the way they stand when they're cold – making fists of their fingers and stuffing them in their pockets. The way they sink their chin to their chest when they're answering an awkward question. And, in the case of Anthony James Duke, the way they wear the collar up on that godforsaken, fleece-lined, red denim jacket.

It could be the wind-chill or it could be me. But I swear the temperature just dropped a full ten degrees C.

CHAPTER SEVEN

I find myself back in the Au Bar, which The Boys and I tracked down last night on a road called, testingly, Eerikinkatu. It was quiet all evening, even when we left about eleven; so much for the prospect of a frenzied Friday night in Helsinki. It's one of the nice things about London that the gay bars get busy early. You can buy a drink and flick through the soft porn masquerading as community journalism without any sense of stigma, because a dozen other blokes are doing it too.

It's different abroad, and I always forget that. Not that I go everywhere with the sole intention of cruising gay bars. I've lost count of the number of times I've walked out of a hotel in a strange town, fully intending to slip into the first hostelry I see; sink a beer amid the local colour, get a taste of the real Paris, Reykjavik, Toronto, Verona ... Except that, as soon as I peer through the window, the local colour always looks flummoxing – so instead, I rerun the same old movie:

> *Open on:* My hand, sliding into back pocket of my jeans. Take out a map and read the annotation: The 'Why-Not?' Bar.

> Hmm! I think, that sounds fun, and it's only two miles away ...

I'm too tight to get a cab and have no intention of mastering another bloody metro, so I head off on foot at a fair old lick. Over the main road, under the underpass, through that poorly lit bit with all the graffiti.

Cut to: Ten minutes later. Scene-change to nowhere I can identify, as I weigh up the relative merits of a) stopping for a squint at the map under a rare working street light thus revealing myself as a muggable tourist; or b) yomping manfully on, body lingo proclaiming I know where I'm going; thus decreasing risk of assault, whilst increasing chance of getting lost and into even greater danger ... Tricky choice, given that the logical outcome of each is waking up in A&E and/or a Terry Gilliam nightmare, with no money, mobile or knowledge of my own name (possibly) and blood group (definitely).

Cut to: Ten minutes further on. I'm now in the red-light district where cars roll slowly by and ladies on corners make unfeasible suggestions. Men try to sell me drugs which, it strikes me, have the same names here as they do at home, making me feel quite patriotic. I fight the urge to stop and gawp into neon-lit sex shops cos I've seen it all before. Except for that video called *Eels for Pleasure*, with its cover that makes me shudder and worry about the teeth.

Fuzzy edit to: The edge of town, where the police presence is heavy enough to alarm and comfort at once. Officers strut about, with firearms belted to jodhpured thighs and an innate sexiness you don't see at home.

Cue sound effects: The rumble of rolling stock and a faraway flash of sparks draw me into the hinterland of a mainline railway station. I'm in an empty street, with peeling posters for obscure charities and a long-gone concert by Celine Dion. Mastery of the street numbering leads me to a door with chipped black paint and a bell to ring for entry. I look around and wonder how I'll ever get back to my hotel. Then I press the buzzer, which emits no audible sound. The locking mechanism groans like a coffee grinder; I push and pull and twist the handle, releasing the catch as the grinding stops. It's even darker inside, and for one last time I think of turning tail and returning to the safer part of town. But that familiar atmosphere of small-city gay bar rises up to greet me like a wet mongrel – and stepping through the wall of stale fag smoke, I'm in.

Cut.

Actually, the Au Bar is nothing like that. It's the other sort of gay bar: bright and splashy, Formica and glass, with wipe-clean tables and comfy sofas. Identikit Europop plays at coffee-hour volume as I settle on a sofa with a beer. I retrieve a leaflet from down the side of the cushion: safer sex tips in Finnish, all moody men and smiley cartoon condoms.

There was no sign of Anthony when I came down from the tower. I walked round to the gates where I'd seen him standing, to find nothing but a squashed Coke can and three dog-ends. I resisted bagging them for analysis, even though they were Marlboro Lights. It was hardly conclusive proof – and anyway, I didn't need it.

I wondered if I could still catch the groundsman, but what would I say?

'*Excuse me, was that my ex you were talking to? The one who trampled my heart to goulash so I never wanted to get close to anyone ever again?*'

I haven't set eyes on Anthony Duke since the day he walked out the second time. Other people have; like Duncan, my best buddy. He's more of a regular around the bars than I am. He's seen him once or twice over the years, but no more than that, which strikes me as odd. The word is that Anthony's still around. He's moved from Vauxhall to Battersea ... taken up with someone he met on the Common ... working at a casino ... being kept by some bloke or other ... The word is never in short supply, but you never know what to believe.

When you split up with someone local, you expect to run into them every other day. You use the same streets, frequent the same shops, clubs, tube stations. In the post-traumatic healing time, the prospect of crossing paths looms over you like a scalpel hell-bent on slicing open your sutures. Just putting out the rubbish becomes a trial; how do you get over someone, how do you put the pain behind you, when they could be walking past your front door?

But you do it. You take out the trash. Fate is rarely as heartless as you fear, and anyway, this is London; I know people living two streets away I don't bump into from one year to the next ... Anyway, I'm fine about him now; enough water's flowed under my bridge since the days of Anthony to refloat a stranded orca. The whole episode made me stronger, and he's been well and truly boxed away. Just not quite the way he deserves.

The Finnish beer is slipping down nicely and I order another. The barman smiles and overdoes the eye-contact thing, which in a straight bar would be just good manners. Here it has a different currency, and the exchange rate can be excellent. But I've never been good at flirting in bars. When I'm nervous, my left arm twitches and I blink too much; it looks like I'm winking when I'm not. Disarming for onlookers plus it's easily misread, so I spend half my time looking at the floor.

The barman is cute in a Nordic way, with psychotically clear blue eyes and cheekbones like sled runners. His style is global-urban; more Hoxton Market than Morten Harket, hair sculpted into peaks like he rubbed it with a balloon. I wonder if I should tip him. That's one thing I always mean to look up before I go abroad; that and whether you can hail a taxi in the street.

I leave a euro on the coaster and sidle back to my sofa. It is Saturday night. The place is already busier than Friday, and the music is cranked up to one notch below the level that requires conversational-yelling. I wonder why I'm not more fazed; here I am, calmly watching the comings and goings of tasty blond tottie, after very nearly running into the man who wrecked my life. And not down the Barrel & Tap – not even in my own country – but a thousand miles from where he should be, on the fringe of the Baltic Sea!

I'm thinking I'll stay for one more beer when I hear a voice above me. His scalp is like coarse-grade sandpaper and he has a goatee beard. He tries again, this time in English.

'Is anyone sitting there?'

'All yours,' I say.

I mean the other seat, but it's open to negotiation. *Tas-ty* ...

He's wearing baggy jeans and a short-sleeved tee with a long-sleeved one underneath. It is a younger man's look, and on him it's just right. (On me, it looks like I got dressed during a fire alarm.) He's still looking my way, and I wonder if there's something going on or he just needs the sit-down.

'Where are you from?' he asks.

'London,' I say, upending the beer into my drying mouth. 'You're from here?'

'No. Turku, but I live in Helsinki now.'

I store that one up in the event of a lull. I'm not originally from London either, but Lancashire seems long ago and never more than now. No one's ever heard of where I was born. The nearest international marker is Liverpool, but as soon as you mention that, people say 'But you haven't got the accent'; usually with a tinge of regret, which I find baffling, because to me that's like saying 'But you haven't got the ebola virus'.

'I'm getting another drink, you want one? My name's Dan, by the way.'

'Magnus,' he replies. Shakes my hand, with a grip which is firm without making a point and drier than mine. 'I'd love one.'

Same barman as before, but if I get eye contact this time I don't notice.

'So what are you doing in Helsinki?' asks Magnus, taking back the hand he left on the seat cushion like it might have blown away.

'Holiday,' I say. 'I'm just here for the weekend. With a couple of mate—'

Shit!

The Boys. We're meant to be having dinner! Now!

'Sorry, Magnus! Would you excuse me a minute …'

Outside, the air is as cold as their voicemail diverts.

Bollocks. This isn't like me. I never forget anything.

This is all sodding Anthony's fault! I only came for a drink to think the whole weird thing through. And maybe – just maybe – because I thought he might be here. Crazy long shot, even in a city this small, but it was at the back of my mind.

So what now? The restaurant was booked for half an hour ago. It'll take me as long again to find a cab and get over there. Time for a text.

HI REALLY SORRY SCREWED UP THE TRAMS. NOT GOING 2 MAKE THE RESTAURANT. WILL GRAB SOMETHING HOT, ARF. C U LATER. MAKE IT UP 2 U PROMISE XX

I select Jack's number and press send. But it's a

feeble signal. The hourglass symbol spins and spins, the texting equivalent of passing a hard motion.

Sod it. I'm in trouble whenever I get back, so rushing will get me nowhere. The Boys are great: adorable, sexy, wild when the mood takes them. But just sometimes, when I do something they don't like, they're a tiny bit like my parents. I can see myself turning up to the restaurant halfway through the meal, to averted eyes and the silent forking of cordon bleu rollmops. And if Phil's been on preheat since we went shopping, this is enough to flip his thermostat to the max.

At last the hourglass disappears, taking my message with it. Back inside the bar, the sofa has been taken by a pair of matching girls in black tops and serious glasses. Magnus has disappeared; but, barring an ice axe through the toilet window, he can't have got out without me seeing.

'For you,' he says, passing me a beer and a smile from just behind the door. We chink, and for the first time I notice how tall he is. Six foot two at least; how absolutely marvellous! I'm a firm believer in the old adage *They're all the same height lying down*. But there's no denying it – I do like tall men.

'Fancy moving on?' says Magnus from way up there.

*

The edges blur at this point, so here's the edited highlights.

Magnus is in e-commerce. A revelation sufficiently un-scintillating to turn my attention to his poky-out chest hair, had it not been there already.

I just really want to shag him.

He takes me to another bar, back in the centre of town. I have two more beers and an uneasy feeling the night is slipping away from me. This new place is unsettling and faintly dreamlike. I felt uneasy from the moment a plaid-clad grizzly insisted I check in my bag and the jacket I'm quite happy wearing. But it's mandatory, according to Magnus.

The bar is packed. I mean really, really packed, with guys in faded jeans and checked shirts. I find it a bit embarrassing; all it needs are the hard hats and a few more moustaches and you could be at a Village People convention. The crowd are dressed the way not-very-clued-up straight people think all gay men dress, and it's all quite strange. And that, let me tell you, is before they start to tango.

Everything stops – even the pool – as couples strut back and forth in time to the music. Hairy forearms brush hairy forearms in a display right out of *Monty Python*. Being a lumberjack may be okay in their eyes, but this is too surreal for me. I start to wonder about Magnus and the sap flowing in his veins. I don't see him fitting in here any more than I do, yet he's swaying to the rhythm, completely at ease. By now our thighs are touching, my navel on a line with the belt buckle discernible through his tees. That's when I notice how narrow his eyebrows are. They stop at the corners of his turned-up eyes, and for the first time I intuit the Inuit in his DNA; a pun which, in my inebriated state, tickles my copywriter's funny bone far more than it deserves.

Call me charitable, but there's nothing I like more than watching uptight straights when they accidentally walk into a gay bar. I love the way they touch each other's sleeve as the truth dawns, and they're forced by decorum to stand their ground and finish their drinks. Except right now I feel like a stranded straight myself. Over the years I've been to some of the sleaziest dives on the planet; yet no amount of black-painted light bulbs and camouflage netting ever made me feel as uneasy as this. I put it down to a combination of alcohol, anxiety and unemployment. And the urge to snog the face off magnificent, magnetic Magnus …

'Don't you like it here?' he asks. He has an ever-so-slightly crooked smile, like Andy Pandy.

'It's fine,' I say. 'It's just, I've never been anywhere qu—'

As his face looms over me like a falling pine our lips make contact. The bristles on his goatee are soft. I want to engulf myself in them, and I'm doing a pretty good job till I ruin it by pulling my head away.

I snatch a mighty breath.

'What's the matter,' he asks, a tiny frown between those teeny eyebrows.

'Nothing,' I say, before going back for more. 'I just forgot to breathe.'

CHAPTER EIGHT

I wake to the familiar feeling of sharing a bed with more than one body. Three to be exact, which should feel more crowded than usual, except I'm in the biggest bed I've ever seen in my life. So big it's more than square; so broad it's wider than it is long. An obsessive-compulsive could have a breakdown deciding where the pillows go.

Morning sun streams through pristine nets as I wonder where I put my watch. Magnus's back is to my right, warm and slightly sticky. On the other side are black velvety jowls and a pair of bloodshot eyes.

Rufus.

I haven't been this close to a boxer dog since I was ten. I used to talk to next door's through a gap in the hedge. Rufus was an ugly beast I felt rather sorry for, if also in awe of his stirringly big black bollocks.

I've no idea what gender this one is; or the other one for that matter, which is wedged between my calves and Magnus's. I remember making a very funny remark ages ago, around 5 a.m., about going to sleep in a pair of boxers. No one laughed, not even Magnus, who was spent and spark out by then. I wonder if I should wake him and try it again. But last night's air of disgruntlement still hangs around, like the thumping in my head and the fetid whiff of poppers.

He hadn't seemed quite so sweet when we got back to wherever we are. I'd disappointed him by saying we couldn't go back to my place, so we ended up here, having another beer downstairs in a sumptuous lounge that felt like a drawing room. All inlaid cabinets and regal portraits. Then he told me in no uncertain terms that it was time for sex. It was hard to act affronted, since I was manoeuvring my head into his lap at the time. My hand had been up his T-shirts the entire cab ride home, but something about his manner had changed. He seemed nervous suddenly, like he didn't want me here, though parts of him clearly did. It was then that Magnus led me up a staircase so winding and gilded I half expected to bump into Fred Astaire coming down. The hounds were in pursuit as we ascended, and for the sake of my libido I was relieved when they collapsed in an obedient heap on the landing. Ask me to get it on under the glare of a dozen sweaty men and I turn into Jeff Stryker; point the gaze of a long-suffering pet in my direction, and the result is an instant marshmallow attack.

The bedchamber was a rococo extravagance. I stood there, trying to take it in, as Magnus stripped off his tops with the steely purpose of a cross-Channel swimmer. Then he keeled over onto the gigantic snowfield of a duvet, hands behind his head. The posture was a challenge: it said *Come on then, if your dick is hard enough …*

That was when I took time-out by shutting myself in the ensuite, trying to unscramble the night. Reality lurched; I felt like I'd been in this bathroom before. But it was just an echo of the one back at the Grand Union Hotel. Same chrome and marble, same expensive toiletries in Terracotta Army formation … (How much do they pay in e-commerce?) And another seed of déjà vu, standing in the tooth mug: two toothbrushes, like when I stowed my own frazzled Oral-B in the hotel bathroom ... So many questions sprang to mind. But even this chillier, arrogant Magnus was too damned irresistible to sidetrack with that sort of probing. I splashed around in the alabaster basin and filched a cap of mouthwash. If there'd been chalk handy, I'd have dusted my palms; I was ready to grapple and this one wasn't getting away.

Now the well-defined back beside me flips over, pale eyes squinting in the light. Magnus is still handsome in the morning, if a bit shiny, and his breath is a definite improvement on the slobbering gale to my left.

It is one of fate's unkinder tricks to bestow on me the raging horn whenever I wake with a hangover. My hand snakes under the duvet to determine the chance of a pre-breakfast resumption of affairs. But before it can complete its mission, a door slams shut downstairs and a bunch of keys drops onto a hard surface. Magnus springs up as if cattle-prodded, levering himself over the bed's most proximate edge.

'You have to go now,' he says charmlessly, slipping into a dressing gown. 'Out through the kitchen. The staff are arriving.'

Any unified show of resistance ebbs away as the dogs abandon ship to claw at the bedroom door. At least some of us are getting breakfast. I dress in silence as Magnus pees loudly with the bathroom door ajar. Retrieving my watch from the shoe where I left it, I realise it's only a quarter past eight. The glands in my neck say I'm very tired.

He hustles me down another staircase that looks like the first one but isn't. Through an eye-level archway halfway down I glimpse another banister, and a black-cuffed hand sliding slowly up it. There is much I haven't fathomed here: about Magnus, and this house with its Escher-configured staircases, wending their way in strange proximity without ever meeting.

'Is that it, then?' I ask, as he sees me off at the back door. His answer is a cursory peck. Then he looks away, exposing our rapacious night for the fraud it was.

I follow the gravel drive back to the road, slightly astonished to find I've still got my new trousers in their Stockmann carrier bag. Pausing at a faux-rustic colonnade, I get a flash recollection: being willingly, drunkenly pinned up against one of its fluted columns only hours before … Magnus was a man in a hurry, right from the off. I feel unsavoury and exhausted as I turn onto the road. I haven't a bloody clue where I am. Downhill, I decide, as the water of the bay and a familiar-looking spire come into view, bathed in subtle light.

Oh God. The hotel's miles away.

I take one last look at the majestic pile where I spent the night. A plaque containing an ornate blue shield is bolted to the wall between two first-floor windows. On either side rear fearsome golden beasts, with sculpted ribbons unfurling about their ankles.

And then I'm smiling – all the way home. Smiling, because all my life I've dreaded that question; the one that comes up when you spend too long drinking with people you hardly know. So next time someone asks, 'So where's the weirdest place you've ever done it?' – I'm ready. I won't have to make up an answer, or come clean about that sad wank into a plastic bag on the train home from a *Doctor Who* convention – *because I've had sex in the back garden of the Dutch Embassy in Helsinki!*

That's good enough for anyone. Even if it was only with the Dutch ambassador's boyfriend; you can always gloss over that.

*

I'm not expecting a great reception at the hotel, and I don't do myself any favours by losing my key card.

One of Phil's eyes and a tuft of spiky fair hair appear round the edge of the door. He says nothing; lets it swing open then hops back into bed. It is like I'm not here. Jack doesn't stir either, so I tiptoe into the bathroom and take a shower. When I come out they're both awake: two solemn heads on the pillow, bedclothes to their chins, like Siamese twins in the school Nativity.

'Where the fuck have you been?' Phil does icy even when he's being funny. This time, he is not being funny.

Just to set the record straight: The Boys and I have never been monogamous, if that's the word. They have their dalliances and I have mine. But anything that happens, happens discreetly. They know as well as I do, what I really need is a boyfriend – as in, a whole one of my own rather than half of two other people's. Not that I always felt this way; for a time, I worried I was becoming too comfortable with Jack and Phil. For the first six months, the frisson of dating not one but two tasty blokes was more than just an ego boost. I felt as happy in their company as I'd felt in anyone's. And since, with them, I had all the pleasures of a boyfriend with none of the granny's-birthday-attending, dry-cleaning-retrieving, dishwasher-leaking drawbacks of real commitment, it was hard to see what I was missing.

The reaction of my friends surprised me, too. No jaws dropped; no one asked for a glass of water. The general consensus was, 'Well, Dan, you've tried everything else, so why not?' Which probably goes to show I'm better at choosing my friends than my lovers. That said, when you secretly think you're being rather saucy, so much broadmindedness is disappointing.

However, in the last couple of months things between The Boys and me have changed. I'm back to trawling the net with my old dry-mouthed enthusiasm. The rule is still 'Don't ask, don't tell', but I reckon we've all felt our relationship drift into the calmer waters of affectionate friendship. All of which ought to make my current predicament easier. Surely?

My left arm is tremoring as I fumble in the drawer for clean underwear, and a ruse to spare me being scimitared into flushable segments by Phil's tongue. Like an idiot, I plump for honesty.

'Look, I'm really sorry about last night. I went home with someone … How was the restaurant?'

'*Sod the fucking restaurant!*' chorus the conjoined actors, with a venom that is less than Christ-like.

'We waited till ten o'clock for you, fella!' says Jack, exasperated.

Now I feel like a real schmuck. Jack never gets angry.

'Ten-a-frigging clock!' spits Phil, who does, all the time.

'In the end the maitre d' said we had to order or go without. You could have called.'

'I did call!' I plead, floundering into pants. 'But your phones were off, so I texted …'

Heads shake in unison, like tennis fans on fast-forward.

'No, you didn't.'

'I did! Didn't you get it?'

I'm looking at Jack.

'Oh aye, that's right!' says Phil, tossing back the bedspread and stamping to the bathroom door. 'It's always Jack, isn't it?' I sense goalposts moving preternaturally, like the trees in *Macbeth*. 'I might have known you'd be messaging him!'

He's quivering as he turns on the threshold. His hands are clamped on either side of the door frame, as if demonstrating good form in an earthquake. I wonder if he's about to hit me.

'Go and have a shower, Phil!' pipes up Jack. He knows the signs.

'I haven't finished yet!' snaps Phil. His tone says, 'You've had this coming'.

I brace myself as he edges towards me. He's in his complimentary bathrobe, I'm in my pants; we look like professional wrestlers in different states of readiness. He stops when his eyebrows are level with mine. I long to tweeze out three mutant strands above his nose, but it's not the time to mention it.

'I am sick of you taking the piss.'

Phew – well, if that's all …

'I am sick of you taking advantage of me's and Jack's good nature!'

His grammar's going. He means business.

'I am sick of the way you treat our home like you own the place … And treat us like shite when we are kind enough to bring you away for the weekend!'

Not strictly true; we're splitting everything three ways, but—

'I am sick of the way you ruin what was *supposed* to

be a nice evening, by sodding off with some bit of trade without having the common courtesy to let us know!'

'I told you, I—'

'Then drag yourself back here when it suits, like a tomcat with its arse bleeding!'

'That'll do, Phil,' says Jack. He's out of bed.

'But above all – I am sick of the way you make it so *painfully frigging obvious* you wish I. Wasn't. Here!'

'Phil, that'll do!'

'I know what you're up to, Dan, you devious gobshite – you want Jack for yourself!'

Uh-oh: unmarked turn into Cloudcuckoosville …

'You've been at it for months, trying to make me feel surplus to requirements!'

That's it – now I'm really lost. And I'm not alone.

'Have a shower, Phil!' says Jack. 'Then you need to start packing.'

He tries to pull him back, but Phil shrugs him off.

'Last night, I told Jack to make a choice – didn't I, Jack?'

'Yes, Phil. When you were pissed …'

'And you chose me – didn't you, Jack?'

I am speechless. This is almost funny. I look to my little mate for support, but he looks away. Just stands there like he's forgotten his lines.

'Oh, come on! You don't believe this, do you, Jack? Phil, you can't mean—'

'Oh, can't I?' he snaps back. 'When we get home, I want you out of our lives … You can take your socks out of our sock drawer. Your porn out of our porn drawer. And you can take your toothbrush out of our toilet bowl, cos that's where you're gonna find it!'

He is edging closer again, chin raised in victory.

'—And I don't want to see you again. Ever. *Goddit?*'

If his nose was any closer, he'd have my eye out. Phil spins on his heel, death blow delivered, and slams the bathroom door.

Jack is staring at the wall. I take a stride towards him, hold out an arm, but he doesn't move.

'Where the fuck did that come from? Jack, he's mad! This is bollocks, you know it is!'

Jack just shakes his head. We're both familiar with Phil's irrational outbursts, and, like me, he usually takes them with a pinch of salt; leave him for long enough and the storm will blow itself out.

But not this time.

'Sorry, Dan,' he says. 'It's for the best.'

Just like that. I slump on the edge of one of the two most expensive beds I've ever slept in.

Then Phil's right; he's won.

'I can't believe you're going along with him,' I say. 'He's barking – this is all in his head! It's …'

For the first time, Jack looks at me.

'He's just scared, Dan. It's for the best. For all of us.' He looks away. 'But you can always leave your porn.'

CHAPTER NINE

Monday is a reality check on all counts.

I'm back in my own bed in Clapham, London SW4. As usual, I wake up two minutes before the alarm. Except my alarm isn't set, because I don't need one, do I?

The sensible side of my brain was hoping I'd make a decision about what to do next while I was in Helsinki. Foolish sensible side! I've done nothing of the sort. So now I'm back I have it all to do, and plenty of time to do it ... A week ago, I had a job and a sort-of-relationship. Today I have neither. Margaret Thatcher and I didn't agree on much, but the woman in the moon was right about one thing: it *is* a funny old world.

Today, I have no distractions and no excuses. As the gentle growl of morning traffic filters through my secondary double glazing, there's not a reason in the world why I shouldn't stay in bed till I've made up my mind. The redundancy payment will be in my bank account by now ... So, Dan, let me ask: Are you really going to fritter it away on one wild, hedonistic summer? Or will you do the sensible thing and get a job before you're desperate for one? Or is it possible you can come up with an amenable combination of the two?

On the one hand, there's something quite poetic about the timing of all this. Today is May 1st; as good as the start of summer, which seems a better time than most to take an unscheduled break from one's career. More than that, at the end of this particular summer stands a milestone; a watershed (what *is* a watershed, and how do you build one?) At the beginning of September, it's my fortieth birthday; an artificial benchmark of nonetheless mystic significance. Ordinarily, I'm not that struck on birthdays, but I daresay I'll let myself get carried along in a bit of forty-fervour when the time comes. It's been at the back of my mind to mark the occasion in some way. Specifically, since the day I emailed everyone I don't dislike and told them to keep the first Saturday in September free.

While we're on the same hand, there's another reason why it makes sense to take a breather now. If my financial adviser has done his sums right (probable) and the pensions market doesn't implode in the interim (less likely), I am halfway through my working life. Turn one way, and I can see the early progress of my career, from my first job flogging theatre tickets in a West End hotel, to my most recent position at Chartwell Shanks. Turn the other way, and I see a long line of question marks stretching into the future, punctuated by the salving of fractious egos and the odd half-decently written advert. This line leads all the way to a gold clock, a fond farewell and a pair of rather elegant slippers.

So why not get off the whirligig for a bit? Recharge my creative batteries, then clamber back on when the nights are drawing in and there's less sunshine to mope at through the office window?

But that's just one side of the argument. On the other hand – on the other hand lies my knob. Quite literally. Irksomely it is standing to, and demanding, attention. As I get out of bed, I know I shouldn't, but I know I'm going to anyway.

Time to log onto the net.

*

In my view, the post-millennium rise of the gay chat room has had two serious casualties. The first is my intake of telly.

I used to be a pretty serious viewer. News, detective dramas, wildlife documentaries and my three favourite soaps. I'd set the video for a week's worth of the latter in case I missed an episode, catching up religiously even if it meant sitting up till 2 a.m. on a school night. Now I don't watch TV much at all, because the net has taught me there is more to life than staring at a screen – ha ha. For example, sex. And that leads me to the second victim of chat-room proliferation: the gay sex club.

I'm less sure about this one, since I don't have a great deal of data to draw upon. But from my odd visits to the Tuesday-night Underwear Party at the Grid, since the rise of click4dick, turnout has been notably down while my pants have stayed upsettingly up. Not a scientific sampling, I grant you, but enough to detect the change.

I've never been a huge fan of your home-grown raunch spot – the kind of place my dear, departed Boys were so fond of. I'm more likely to indulge when on holiday; like trains, they do sex clubs so much better abroad. There's nothing more miserable than a gay sauna full of Brits. If I go, it's always the wrong time of day: just me, a few old blokes and a small but eager Asian gentleman.

Even pre-net, even when I was young, copping off in those establishments wasn't my thing, any more than pulling men in bars. I lacked the knack, the look, the luck or the pheromones to be irresistible. Nowadays I also lack the laxity, because the older I get, the less inclined I am to settle for just anyone. I'll set my sights on some stunner in a crisp white towel, aware that my efforts to engage him in full-body contact will be futile. Advances spurned so pointedly you'd think I was slinking around with a dead pigeon on my head, I will leave unsated; usually catching sight of him copping off with someone gorgeous just as I'm shrugging huffily into my streetwear.

And so it came to pass that I discovered click4dick.

*

Without opening the sitting-room curtains I slump down at the desk. I'm sipping my morning Earl Grey from its customary mug, festooned with beefy Aussie Rules footballers. The laptop grinds its way online, then I enter my name and password into click4dick.com.

HORNYDSW4 has three new messages. All left since he logged off last night.

> *MAN4UTOOT 00:55, April 30*
> *Hi handsome nice pics. You looking 4 a meet*
> *now? My place only.*
> *[1] [2]*

> *QUETZAL 01:01, April 30*
> *Have I see you somewhere. Do you go Exodus.*

> *GR8GEEZER 01:26, April 30*
> *ALLO MATE STILL IGNORIN ME THEN.*
> *WHEN WE GOIN FOR THAT BEER, LICK*
> *LICK **CHEEKY GRIN***
> *[1]*

I take a look at their profiles, and in the case of MAN4UTOOT and GR8GEEZER, click on the extra pictures attached to their messages.

MAN4UTOOT, as his screen name implies, lives in Tooting, which is just down the road. That explains why he was targeting me late at night: the distance your average click4dick-er will travel for gratification diminishes with the lateness of the hour. I was asleep before his message came through but, judging by the beer belly hanging over his football shorts, it is not an opportunity I'd have braved the night for. His supplementary pics are predictable; they document the contents of said shorts, which are nothing to write home about unless your mother has a penchant for intimate jewellery.

GR8GEEZER I have come across before. I took a bit of a shine to him in my early days online. His real name is Wayne, and he basks in his heritage as a genuine East End lad. He is twenty-eight, with cropped hair and sexy, arrogant lips. In his profile blurb he portrays himself as a rough diamond who lives on the edge and just happens to be gay. The 'occupation' box is left blank, which usually means they're unemployed or cabin crew. He has recently replaced some rather fuzzy scans with a nice set of digital photos. In them he is standing in a deserted alley, one Doc Marten up on a wall amid slanting sun rays. It's a decent attempt at gritty Deptford reportage. Except when you've spent as many hours clicking profiles as I have, the set-up looks familiar. A handful of guys on click4dick offer photographic services to the rest of the membership, so consequently the same old locales and backdrops pop up again and again. That alley, I happen to know, is just off Hampstead High Street, and the shots are angled to avoid the frontage of a very chi-chi milliner's.

GR8GEEZER's more candid shots are taken indoors. Nothing too graphic: just a bit of geezery topless flesh with the waistband of his trackie bottoms slouching beneath eminently kissable hip bones. His torso is smooth and well defined. Sexy because it looks natural, the result of just the right amount of gym work or maddeningly lucky genetics. Or, as he'd have you believe, long and raucous days spent dismantling scaffolding. He and I have swapped messages many times, though we've never met. I've suggested it on three occasions but he's never followed through. He would always '*love to mate, but …*' The excuse is either that he's '*goin' out to give it large*', '*hooking up wiv me mates to watch the match*', or '*gonna see a man about a dog*'.

(Please …)

He is clearly a cod-Cockney, and a cock-teaser to boot. You get a lot of that online. And, since I've grown wise to him, the Doc Marten is now on the other foot. He's all over me like a rash. Or at least, he's the one making the overtures which I've so far ignored. I'm quite sure he's all mouth and no trouser snake, despite a growing body of evidence to the contrary; ever since I started played it cool, he's been sending me his more revealing private pics.

I click on his latest attachment and wait for it to open. It is a close-up of a pair of agreeably well-filled blue Speedos shot from above, which means it's a self-portrait. The contents are a cuppable handful; not what you'd call aquatically streamlined, nor necessarily his at all. What you see online isn't always what you get – and everyone you meet has a story about that.

I give QUETZAL a cursory look. He is South American, a mite pouty with bouffant hair. Not my type, particularly if he hangs out at clubs like the Exodus. That's a West End favourite of the cooler clubbing set, all hard house and nosebleed techno, or whatever the tuneless bleeps they're knocking their drugs back to these days. A couple of pints and a shuffle to Kylie at the Barrel & Tap is more me, so I doubt I'd have much to say to QUETZAL. But then on a website like this, conversation is rarely top of the agenda.

As if to contradict me, at that moment a new message pops up from another familiar name.

> *MAESTROMAN 08:55, May 1*
> *Hi Dan. Hope you're bearing up after the bad*
> *news at work. How was Hell's Kinki and did it*
> *live up to its name?!*

MAESTROMAN and I are net buddies. We've never actually met. He messaged me with something witty ages ago and we hit it off. He's one of those guys with no pictures on his profile, which I've never understood. But since my sole purpose for being on here is to get laid, I guess I wouldn't, would I?

MAESTROMAN is cagey. He has never told me his name or much about himself, though the fact he logs onto the South London page implies he's local. I don't normally bother with guys if they haven't got pictures. You've no idea who you're talking to, and they mostly just want to swap smutty messages like a cumbersome sort of phone sex. Chances are they're seventy-odd, in or halfway out of smelly trousers, which doesn't do it for me. My charity ends at a standing order to Greenpeace.

And yet, through a combination of making me laugh and being a sturdy if intangible shoulder to cry on, Mr Maestro has become a good friend. We never talk dirty. Or not since the night I got in from the pub, pissed and horny. That's the worst time to go online; when I'm most likely to hook up with someone I know nothing about and get in a cab to nowhere I know. Or worse, invite them round here. It turned out MAESTROMAN was rather good at cyber smutty talk. He has an excellent vocabulary, including a firm grip on the sleazy end of the dictionary. I think we were both a bit embarrassed afterwards, because we didn't chat again for weeks. And that bothered me, sullying our intimacy with all that tacky shit. It hasn't been mentioned, but now we're back to our old supportive ways. Or at least, he supports me; he doesn't talk about himself much. I know he's a musician and quite a successful one. Hence MAESTROMAN, his online persona. A bit self-congratulatory perhaps, but I've resisted asking if he can blow his own trumpet.

I send him a reply.

> *HORNYDSW4 08:57, May 1*
> *wotcha maestro. fine here thanx. still mulling over options re work. helsinki was fun, tho I did get the heave-ho from the boys …*

He is back, quick as a flash.

> *MAESTROMAN 08:58, May 1*
> *Sorry to hear that, Dan. What you'd call a finnish finish then. Is the situation retrievable or is it back to the message board?!*

HORNYDSW4 09:00, May 1
arf. finnish finish. v good. no, I reckon that's
that for the chewsome twosome. been fun, but it
was never going anywhere. how was your
weekend?

MAESTROMAN 9:03, May 1
Weekend good if uneventful. Lots of practice.
Got a tough new piece to learn and it's taking a
while. Chin up re the boys. What went wrong,
may I ask?

HORNYDSW4 09:07, May 1
all a bit mad, maestro. and kind of inevitable i
suppose. guess threesomes tend to fall apart
when one half of the couple decides the
interloper prefers the other half over him. think
that's what happened, if u get my drift.

MAESTROMAN 09:08, May 1
Crystalline as ever, Dan. Still, sounds like you
had fun while it lasted …

HORNYDSW4 09:10, May 1
yeah, u know. fun schmun. it was never the real
world, eh. talking of which, what are u
rehearsing for? something I can come to – try
and spot u amid the musos, oh man of mystery?
arf …

This is a long shot. Mr Maestro has never been keen on meeting and he's never told me why. According to the scant info on his profile, he is tall, dark and thirty-eight, which could be right up my alley. But much as I like the sound of him, something makes me wary. He's happy being net buddies and I am too. Click4dick is a shallow, seductive cesspool, so it's a relief when the occasional voice of reason bobs to the surface. Besides, if he *is* a blow-waved granddad, hunched one-handed over his keyboard in Peckham, I'd rather not know.

> *MAESTROMAN 09:16, May 1*
> *LOL. Not sure about that one. Have to see if my performance merits your presence. Anyway, better scoot. Got a rehearsal, and I was late for the last one. My car gave up the ghost and I had to get public transport – bit like your love life really …*

> *HORNYDSW4 09:17, May 1*
> *you lost me …*

> *MAESTROMAN 09:19, May 1*
> *I waited ages, then two buses came at once …*
> *Catch you later. MM XX*

Very droll … I'm just thinking about making another cuppa before I trawl through the 'Who's begging for it a condom's toss from my house' page, when my mobile chirps. It's a text from Duncan.

> HI BABE. FANCY CATCHING UP? WILL
> BE YOUR WAY ONE PM. COULD GRAB
> A BITE TO EAT … PS WELCOME TO THE
> LAND OF LADIES WOT LUNCH! D X

Now that's a good way of thinking about it. Time off in the week is a rare and wonderful thing when you're a nine-to-fiver. You get used to cramming your shopping and seeing your mates into the precious hours outside work. But not all my friends are easy to pin down: young mums with broods to bath – even Duncan. He's a medium-sized shot in healthcare, always putting in extra shifts or off on a training weekend; and that's when he's not working on his PhD. He's been studying since the day we met, and his drive is boundless. He works four long shifts a week at the hospital, at a pace that would send your average overpaid advertising type whinging to their headhunter. Then he has Fridays off to study.

I text back and suggest the little pizzeria on my road. It's half-price before 5 p.m. I'm just wondering what to do until then, when up flashes another message.

SLINGSTUD24 09:32, May 1
Hi mate. You look well tasty. Looking for a
horny meet before 2pm. In Stockwell can accom
or travel. What you into?

A quick flick through his pics and … Blimey, I've never seen him before! He's got amazing equipment, and I don't mean the anatomical sort. In most of his photos he's lying down, suspended in what looks like a hammock designed by the Marquis de Sade. He takes his role play seriously, judging by the grimace visible through the gap in his black leather mask. Going by the one pic where you can actually see his face, he's not bad looking.

I'm in the mood for adventure. And I've got nothing

else to do before lunch, so I click reply. As ever with click4dick, a fast response is everything – and anyway, it's a shame to leave him dangling …

CHAPTER TEN

Duncan is half an hour late, but one glimpse of his cheery smile and it is impossible to mind. His smart white shirt, untucked over black jeans, is accessorised with cufflinks that read *TOP* and *BOTTOM*.

'I can't believe the traffic,' he says, pouring himself a mineral water, 'and I had to return that birthday gift I bought my goddaughter. It was cowhide, and you know her dad's gone vegan … Have you ordered?'

Dunc is my best friend in the world. Originally from Glasgow, he's been living in London as long as I have. We met in a club eight years ago and had a catastrophic one-night stand. I fell asleep on the job and dribbled into his pillow all night. He had the grace to see the funny side, and gave me a lift home in the morning. We've been buddies ever since.

'Talking of cowhide, how was the leather boy?'

Duncan and I are both on click4dick. For the sake of security, we always text each other when we're meeting someone new.

'Yeah, not bad,' I say, opening the pizza menu. 'He lives in one of those tower blocks in Stockwell with the panoramic views. Spare room's a dungeon: rubber groundsheet, loads of candles …'

'I know, I saw the pictures. Got a sling and everything … Did you have a go in it?'

I tut. 'Of course I didn't!' Duncan knows I have an invisible No Entry sign tattooed on my arse. 'Not that I could have got him out of it …'

His eyes gape as he crunches a breadstick. 'Was he total bottom? How fantastic. I might message him myself.'

'Do. But be warned, once he's strapped in he can see all the way to the Embankment, and he knows the name of every sodding building. Are you having a starter?'

We decide on a pizza each and a salad to share. Duncan is vegetarian, for reasons lost in the mists of time. Which is fine in a place like this, though when we've been on holiday in Spain or the more backward bits of America, his options are limited. By day three he's usually got omelette coming out of his ears, which does his cholesterol levels no favours at all. You see, Duncan is big – in click4dick-speak, *rugby build*, though you wouldn't bet on him in a sprint for the touchline.

'How are you feeling today, honey?' he asks. 'Big changes in your life …'

He was the first person I called when the axe fell at Chartwell Shanks. Duncan doesn't get the nuances of ad-agency politics, any more than I can follow the finer points of evidence-based practice in coronary care. It doesn't seem to matter; we've both learned to listen and nod in the right places. He was also the first person I called when I got in from the airport last night.

'It's funny,' I say. 'I feel like I'm having a new leaf turned over for me whether I want it or not. As for losing my job – well, I've done the sums. If I don't go mad, I can afford to take the summer off and worry about work after my birthday!'

At that moment the waiter arrives with our food. He swings down the pizzas from shoulder height, plonking them on the wipe-clean gingham. Then he whips out the pepper mill from the back pocket of his jeans, brandishing it with a nonchalance I can feel down to my toes. This particular waiter has worked here for years. He's genuine Italian, very straight, with thick black hair and eyebrows like the soft side of Velcro. And he never, ever smiles. You just know that if you were his bitch, he would take you roughly from behind and gob in your hair at the point of orgasm.

Duncan and I love him. We call him Deadpan Pizza Man.

'Thanks,' says Dunc; then, wistfully to his retreating back: 'We still on for that date … ?'

In the evenings it's always heaving in here. The food is great, and cheap even at full price. The place has the whiff of Italian authenticity, right down to the telly showing football in the alcove. The chairs clatter on the tiles when you sit down; the pizzas are loaded and crispy, big as dustbin lids. But now only three other tables are taken. Mums 'n' pushchairs on two, plus an old boy with his newspaper at the back. It's a different environment, this work-free world.

Duncan takes a bite of his favourite quattro formaggi ('Cabbage diet next week, so what the hell?'). His eyes roll blissfully back into his head.

'Mmmm … So what about Sandra? What's she going to do?'

'Not sure,' I say. 'That's a bridge we haven't crossed yet. We agreed we're going to talk in a week or two. If I know her, she'll be dying to get back on the chain gang. Different priorities, but – well, that's her problem, I'm afraid … And she's as much chance of finding something on her own as she has with me, anyway.' Duncan is looking me in the eye; I suspect I sound like a schmuck. 'Am I being terrible?'

He considers a moment. 'No. You've got to look after numero uno. Everyone's entitled to take a break if they get the chance … And anyway,' he says, biting through a lava flow of ricotta, 'you can help me find a flat.'

Now this is news! Duncan breaks into a big smile.

'I finally agreed the settlement with Colin. He says he can transfer me the money first week of June!'

'Brilliant! How much?'

He tells me. There's a lot to be said for reaching an amicable settlement with your rich ex-boyfriend-cum-landlord. And I thought my redundancy was a hefty whack …

'Pudding's on me,' he says, as the Lambrusco Lothario collects up our plates.

Duncan tries to catch his eye. 'Can we see the dessert menu?'

Not a chance.

'Tiramisu,' he growls. 'Or crème caramel.'

It's more an ultimatum than a choice. And that's when it comes to me in a flash – what it is that makes this waiter so incredibly hot.

He's got Virgil Tracy's eyebrows!

Virgil Tracy was the puppet that piloted Thunderbird Two when I was a kid. He was also the first person I ever fancied, which is less unsavoury than its sounds, given that we were both under four foot tall at the time. What *is* a bit kinky is that the thought of him still juices me up to this day. All it takes is an echo of those mink-soft, caterpillar eyebrows, which do for me what Bette Davis's eyes did for whoever wrote that song.

'*Dan?*'

'Sorry …' I gather myself with a sip of water. 'I'll have the tiramisu.'

'Two tiramisus,' monotones the waiter, loping away.

Duncan is de-shining his forehead on a paper napkin as he watches him go. 'Is he the sexiest man you've ever seen in your life, or what?'

I slap a hand to my own forehead.

'God, Dunc – that reminds me!'

How on earth could I forget a titbit like this?

'You will not believe who I saw in Helsinki …'

CHAPTER ELEVEN

The next week I spend on the housekeeping of life.

I remember my mum's wise words – the ones about not leaving your homework till Sunday night. So I get on with updating my portfolio before I need it, looking out the proofs of any decent ads I squirrelled away while I was still at work. I mount them on card, then snap them into the big leather binder that tells the tale of my moderately successful career in advertising, ready for the day of doom when I'm back on the interview circuit.

By rights, every ad should be printed in bile for all the angst that went into it: the stacks of rejected concepts, the wittier headlines that ended up in the bin, the comments from clients that made you want to grab the nearest Apple Mac and hurl it through the window. But already the ads seem of little consequence; as subliminal to me as they were to the million newspaper readers who turned the page without even noticing. I thought I'd miss the buzz of the biz – the frenzied rewrites, the addictive pressure to come up with a better idea quicker than the team next door – but I don't. I don't miss any of it. Just the puns, maybe.

I get a man in to cure my video of its dodgy tracking. And another to look at my washing machine, which has taken to siphoning back litres of dirty water it's meant to spin away. The problem's been plaguing me for months, causing a fetid odour to visit my kitchen, to the point where I've begun to think of my Hotpoint as the demonic relation of those limestone Madonnas that weep semi-skimmed milk. I'm on the verge of calling an exorcist, until Barry from Balham deduces that tightening the junction cap is just as effective.

I visit the gym. I swim at the pool. I also nip into town for lunch with Gina, and through her I get a little fix of office life. She works in marketing at the National Theatre, which makes her good for gossip from in front, behind and either side of the curtain.

And I have sex, I'm afraid. Three or four times, none of them memorable. I think it was Sophocles who said the urge to have sex is like being chained to a lunatic. I'm with him on that one. Half the time it's just a damn nuisance – an impulse I'm hoping fizzles out as the years roll on. Sometimes I long for the day when I'm propped up on my special pillow, with a packet of Fig Rolls all to myself; when some saucy young buck in a nurse's uniform walks in with a flannel and a cheery wink and says, 'Morning, Dan – ready for your bed bath?'; and my first thought is whether he'll be done in time for *Trisha* on the Vintage Channel.

For a while, I was pretty sure the itch was diminishing. These days I'm less likely to queue at the checkout with a trolley full of unwanted groceries, eyes glued to the back of a sinuous neck. And I don't play Escalator Head nearly as much as I used to. That's where you're coming up the escalator from the tube, and you have to pick someone to go down on from all the people travelling the other way. It's a game of skill and tactics because you only get one go, so if you've already chosen and someone cuter comes along, it's tough shit. The defining rule of Escalator Head is that if you do reach the end without choosing anyone, you're honour-bound to imagine servicing whoever's on the top step. It's silly, sometimes arousing, and can be educational. I learned that guide dogs always step on *after* their handler from playing Escalator Head.

But now, with time on my hands and the net at my fingertips, the itch is back. And I'm worried; I can see myself squandering great gaping tracts of this summer staring into cyberspace. Sat here, dangling my bait, like those sad little anglers clustered round the duck pond on the Common.

Click4dick is a dangerous drug. We all know it. We all share it. As a demographic, gay men are thrilled by the cutting edge of anything, particularly where they muster in cities. You only have to check out the 'Online Now' page to see the evidence. Log on in the middle of the night and you'll find thousands of guys in London, hundreds in Manchester or Glasgow, and two men and a goldfish in Batley. Click4dick is available 24/7. And that makes two of us, because these days I'm part of the melee anytime I like. Chatting, flirting, negotiating, without the threat of Lionel Shanks snooping over my shoulder to make me whip it off the screen.

Now I have my drug on tap. I've died and gone to junkie heaven. Except that what I really need is a saviour. A boyfriend, to forgive me all of my trespasses and lead me not into temptation.

A-man.

*

As if my leisurely status wasn't wonderful enough, the weather conspires to make it even better. My mum's other adage, about ne'er casting a clout till May is out, proves unwarranted. The sun shines agreeably for the best part of a month, and clout-wise I'm getting along fine in shorts and T-shirts. I have to keep reminding myself this is really happening. At first, I was getting sympathetic emails from Lalita and the guys at work. These soon tailed off once we all realised it wasn't me who deserved the sympathy.

Of course, harsh reality intrudes now and again – like signing-on day. I haven't been inside a job centre since I was a student, and I'm expecting something grim. My abiding memories of signing-on are a queue of grey-faced people and an air of utter hopelessness. That was during university holidays when I was back home in Lancashire, under my parents' wing. I also felt a bit of a fraud for being there, and I feel the same now. I've got money in the bank, a relatively small mortgage. But I've hardened over the years; if you're entitled to it, you may as well have it.

It's been exactly three weeks since I got the chop. I've sent back all the forms and now I'm ready to sign on for the first time. It'll be a month before I get any dole or whatever it's called these days. But rules are rules, so I take my attendance card and walk across the Common. It is a ritual I am to repeat at 11 a.m. on alternate Thursdays for the rest of the summer.

The local job centre is in an imposing building called Admiralty House. It has a whisper of the neo-Gothic, and a bellow of the sea. On the parapet over the door a sculpted ship's prow emerges from the brickwork, like a baby frozen in mid-delivery. On either side are fearsome whales; the kind you see on ancient maritime charts, with incongruous scales and the face of Orville the Duck on crack. Like them, the building doesn't quite belong. It would look more at ease by the ocean, instead of over the road from an urban green space. But if Al Gore's right about the glaciers, it'll look spot-on when the Thames floods London.

Through the doors at the top of the steps are a battalion of security guards – a man and two women in smart grey uniforms, pacing around on watch. It's brighter and more inviting than the dole office I remember. Except it's not a dole office now. Or even a job centre. As every poster, dividing screen and sticker points out, this is a *Jobcentre Plus*. (Who thinks up this crap? Oh – people like me.)

The waiting area is corralled by a horseshoe of workstations which act as signing-on points. Half of them are empty, I note, as I park myself on the modular seating. My chair has a little laminate armrest, just the size for a cocktail. The place is decked out in primary-school colours – lemon and orange, with concealed ceiling lights. At the back are big windows, and a view of a leafy quadrangle where brocaded sailors might once have strolled.

Everything is quiet and well-ordered, and the place stinks of design agency re-brand. It's all breathlessly ergonomic, from the kidney-shaped desks to the touchscreen information points like aerodynamic tumble dryers. Any pesky buttons they haven't managed to rationalise away have finger-shaped depressions – a pointer, perhaps, to anyone minded to try operating them with a buttock.

The staff are less state-of-the-art. There's a very pretty black girl, called Ferrone. She is small and immaculately dressed. Over the summer I never see her with the same hairstyle twice. Getting it done must take up her entire weekend, but then every day is Sunday in Ferrone's world. She processes her punters at a leisurely pace with due respect for her nails. There's something quite therapeutic about watching her work, like gazing into a lava lamp. That said, I'm grateful not to be allotted to her care; give it a few weeks, and I can see myself trying to bludgeon some urgency into her with one of her kitten heels.

Then there's a couple of lads who slouch about like wearing a tie is killing them. For this they have my sympathy; not having to wear a suit is one of the best things about my job. I've always prided myself on not owning one, bar a cheap tux. Even that I blagged on expenses years ago, to pick up an award for 'Best Integrated Customer-Focused Business-to-Business Campaign (Financial)'. As I said at the time, you need to look the part when you're mixing with the elite.

Over in the corner there's an older bloke in shirtsleeves, who seems to be the supervisor. He looks permanently startled and in need of a fag, like the figure on the bridge in *The Scream*. Then beside him there's Viv – queen of Signing-On Point Two. And she's my girl.

Viv is one of those people whose age is difficult to gauge. She could be forty or she could be sixty. She has no discernible waist, and bosoms like discarded sandbags. I'm to learn a lot about her as the weeks unfold. More than she imagines. You can pick up a lot about someone while you're waiting your turn to sign, particularly when they take personal phone calls. Viv drives into London from Egham, where she lives with her daughter and a cat; they holiday in Florida, and sing in the local operatic society where Viv also does the costumes.

When the girl in front of me vacates the signing-on seat, I take her place as per procedure. Viv rounds up the complexities of this last transaction before appearing to notice me.

'Morning!' she says, slightly startled, like my presence is unexpected.

I hand over my attendance card and she types in my National Insurance number. She blinks through sturdy-framed glasses which might have been her husband's.

'How are you, then?' she asks suddenly, as if the 'Being Cheery' unit of her Customer Care course came back to her with a jolt.

'Fine, thanks,' I say, trying not to appear too fine. If I'm to carry off the pretence of seeking work for three months, I should start now.

Viv fishes in her card index and pulls out my details. As I sign and date the first of many boxes, she peers at the computer as if through a misted windscreen. The particulars of the kind of job I'm pretending to want have found their way onto her PC. She is duty-bound to inform me of any suitable vacancies, and something has caught her eye. She reads it again over the top of her glasses.

'I don't suppose you speak Tamil?' she says, breaking into a grin that brings to mind a vandalised cemetery.

'I don't, I'm afraid. Why?'

'There's a job for a publicity copywriter in local government. But you'd have to speak Tamil …' She scrolls down. 'You'd also have to relocate to Bristol.'

We agree I can probably skirt the poverty trap a week or two longer. Who knows if the sun's shining in Bristol?

*

I moved to Clapham ten years ago. Before that, I lived in Streatham and Wandsworth. It's true what they say about North and South Londoners sticking to their manor. Nearly all my friends live south of the river and, work aside, I rarely have reason to venture north. One of the key reasons for buying my flat was its proximity to the tube. I'm two minutes from the station, on the middle floor of a Victorian end-of-terrace above a drycleaner's. Some nights, when I'm in bed after the station has shut, I can hear the trains rumbling underground like unquiet spectres. The other reason for choosing my flat was Clapham Common, of which I have an uninterrupted view from my sitting-room. Or I do if you sit on the floor, thus obscuring the lamp posts and the double-decker buses that plough up and down the five lanes dividing me from it. To tell you the truth, the traffic doesn't bother me. My sort-of double glazing suppresses it to a sound like the sea: urban womb music that lulls me to sleep at night, drowsily content that at least there's someone around. I can't speak for the flat, but for me it was love at first sight. I was ninety per cent sure we were meant for each other before I was even through the door. Whatever happened to the property market, the flat would always be on a corner, near the tube, overlooking the Common. Location, location, location.

For the first nine years I didn't think much of Clapham Common itself. It was the equivalent of a Dickensian urchin; always there outside my window and not as clean as it could be. I'd sunbathe on it now and again, and occasionally, pre-internet, visit its notorious cruising ground after a hapless night at the Barrel & Tap. But now that I have the days to myself, I am discovering the breadth of its charms. Its great green expanse is my favourite detour to and from the high-street shops, the cinema and, today, the Jobcentre Plus. Strange to think, in all these years I've only ever been on the Common at weekends, at least in daylight. On Saturdays and Sundays, when the sun shines its acres are heaving, with boozers from the Windmill, families with toddlers, footballers, softballers, cricketers and rugger boys.

But on weekdays, before the schools break up, there's hardly anyone around. As I amble back from signing on, truants trundle round the rickety skate park. Crows strut across the grass, glossy and alarmingly large, heads shuffling back and forth like sand-dancing pallbearers. The clouds are low but friendly, and they change formation at speed. First they're a choppy sea that merges into mountainous ridges. They've coalesced into a shark's fin as I spot a familiar figure in the distance: a chocolate-brown Labrador I see two or three times a week. She and her owner have been passing my window for months, and I've watched her grow from unruly pup to obedient princess. Today is a treat: she has two walkers, who take it in turns to throw a stick and pretend they can reach it before her. If I ever have a dog, I want one like her.

I pass the bandstand and the ancient café, where, according to the hoarding, you can take your pick from '*Coffee &* '. On one of the benches a bluff old boy with a bright-red face is taking the weight off. He's got his eye on three assorted mutts of his own as they snuffle and cavort at his feet. He fell asleep in the sun yesterday, I reckon. Or spent it in the pub.

Past the fenced-off playground and I'm nearly home. Two dads chat dutifully by the roundabout, in deference to a stern notice about *Parents Accompanying Children*. A smattering of pre-school kids are climbing frames and riding seesaws, sullenly unobserved. Further on, beyond the duck pond, is a terrace of fine gabled townhouses I've passed a hundred times and never noticed. The way they seem to rise from the water they're a little piece of Amsterdam, I think, as I pass the gentlemen's toilets; which have a reputation for being another. One window is cracked, and covered by yet another imperious warning from the council:

NO LOITERING.
PREMISES UNDER CONSTANT SURVEILLANCE.

If that isn't dangling a carrot for the local exhibitionists, I don't know what is.

High in the sky, the shark's fin has given up its illusion of substance. It re-forms into a puff of smoke amid the sun rays – then disperses to nothing as a shiny, silent minnow flies through it en route to Heathrow.

CHAPTER TWELVE

I'm determined not to let my fitness regime slip, just because I haven't got a job to run away from. When I was working I was a regular at my gym – a small but serviceable branch of New York Fitness, under a hair salon five minutes from the office. Sandra and I had snapped up corporate membership on our first day at Chartwell Shanks – all part of Denzil Wilkes's irresistible package. Denzil was head of Personnel as well as finance director, so I'd have probably bought meteor-strike insurance if he'd been offering it.

I've been a dedicated gym bunny since I was the greenest of budding copywriters. I heard the siren-call of the pub in my first days in the business, one that my fellow creatives answered every lunchtime. Once I realised joining them would send the girth of my wallet and waistline in opposite directions, I needed a displacement activity. That led me to my first gym in Covent Garden – a lofty but oppressive place which reeked of sweaty exertion. One day a pigeon fluttered in from the Piazza, roosting on a girder before falling dead to the floor. Asphyxiation, at a guess; since hot air rises, it had to be ten times stinkier up there.

From then on, I've always found a gym within walking distance of work. Keeping up the routine comes easily to me. I like the primal challenge of the weights, and the stretches keep a lid on my grumbling RSI, for which I blame too much mouse-work. When I teamed up with Sandra, it turned out she was a believer too. A bonus: you can do without an art director raising eyebrows at you when you're late back from your shower. Particularly when they reek of alcohol and can hardly keep their layout pad in focus.

I've kept up my gym membership for now. It's a good deal and it gets me out of the flat. But for days when I don't feel like trekking into the centre of London, I've discovered an option closer to home: Clapham's municipal swimming baths. They're just off the high street and a bit of a sorry sight. None of the cash lavished on a recent refit trickled down to the pool. Or its musty changing rooms, where a notice says that facilities are checked regularly for hygiene, despite a distinctive pube which has picketed the end urinal for a week.

The only time the pool gets busy is when twenty local ladies go for the burn in aqua aerobics. They're accompanied by a male instructor in a polo shirt, who strides about on the side yelling like Busby Berkeley on a very low-budget movie set. But the silence from outside tells me there's no class today. I choose a locker and slip into my trunks, then take the obligatory pre-swim shower to chill the body temperature in preparation for what lies beyond the frothy rock pool of the verruca trough.

I plunge into the lane reserved exclusively for fast swimmers. I'm proud to say I qualify, though as a rule the competition isn't fierce. I do the first of my sixty laps – thirty front crawl, thirty breaststroke – on a single breath and using just my arms, for the same reason dogs lick their balls. My crawl technique isn't great – lots of arms and not many legs – but it's effective.

Halfway through, I switch to breaststroke. I'm starting to flag, so I avoid swimming into the inlet jets at the end that make me feel like a weary salmon. That's when I glimpse the girl in an orange one-piece sashaying out of the changing room. She takes the medium lane, plopping into the water a length behind me. She's slim, with a nose clip, tinted goggles and water-resistant earplugs. There's something pervy about all that sensory deprivation, but she means business all right.

Six lengths from home, I'm tiring fast. I'd sigh if it wasn't medically inadvisable, because I hate being overtaken by girls. Pathetic, I know, and all down to getting thrashed at cross-country by half the netball team. As I push off the deep end she's not far behind. I wonder if she knows I'm trying to keep ahead, or if this is a duel of my own making.

Next lap, she's gaining ground. Half a length has shrunk to five metres. Her crawl technique is serene, each stroke long and economical with a generous payoff for energy expended. I think about sharks – the way they propel themselves with barely a fin-flick.

Two lengths to go and we're almost side by side. I push off like a startled frog as she tumble-turns – that thing I've never mastered. When she breaks the surface again we're parallel, separated only by the lane divider. I come into the wall for the final time; turn, spring, think marlin-sleekness as I visualise myself slicing through the water … But the exertion dislodges my goggles, the left lens filling with water as the elastic cuts into my ear. My form deserts me with six metres to go, and as I lunge for the tiles she does another perfect tumble and pulls away in a streak of orange. For a minute I hang there, panting. Then I splatter back to the changing rooms without a backward glance.

Second time round, the shower feels warmer. I'm dechlorinating in its insipid flow when I hear voices in the locker area. Except it's just one voice. I peek round the communal stall; a guy in his twenties is unpacking his stuff on the bench, talking on a hands-free mobile; something to do with second-quarter retail projections and how they compare with last year. But he isn't on a mobile, and he doesn't look like a businessman. He's grungy with unkempt hair, like he woke up under a tree at Glastonbury. He's still babbling as he takes his shirt off, slinging it in the locker with an irate remark about head office in Aldershot.

As I'm drying myself, I wonder if he's okay to be out alone. He turns back to the locker, and that's when I see his tattoo – faded colours filling a blue-black outline: Tintin and his little dog Snowy, peeping playfully from his shoulder blade.

Exactly where Anthony had the same tattoo.

I can't tell if I'm twitching or shivering. I put it down to being half-naked in a draught. The guy picks up his towel and whips past me in his crumpled surf shorts, deep in conference about the recent dip in sales.

As I make my way out, the side door to the pool is ajar. There he is in the fast lane, head held clear of the water, swimming a pedestrian breaststroke that would get him relegated to the slow one on a busy day. Assuming you could get a word in: he's still talking. Orangina's there too, gliding up and down in her earplugs, oblivious.

Odd. I've only ever seen that tattoo on two people and I doubted the sanity of them both. I pass a door that says 'Girls Changing', which strikes me as a provocation to perverts on at least two levels.

And that's when I wonder if they're both fine, and it's me who's weird after all.

CHAPTER THIRTEEN

Anthony hasn't been in my head for years. His return is not welcome.

At the time, he was Virgil Tracy to the power of – of love, I suppose. He was the first man I ever fell head-over-heels for, the one that showed up all my previous peccadilloes for what they were. The way we met was odd. It was a Saturday night in summer, not long after I'd met Duncan. He and I were big buddies already, the memory of our disastrous fling washed away in a growing swell of friendship. I know it was Saturday, because I did something completely out of character – I went out clubbing two nights on the trot to the same venue.

Wallops was South West London's premier gay disco cellar, opposite the ice rink in Streatham. Long gone now, it was a regular haunt of ours back then, and this particular Friday night had been a great success. I pulled a traffic warden from Crystal Palace called Grant, which in its way was a dream come true. Like half the man-fancying world, I have a thing for men in uniform, and he was as close as I'd got. Not that he was wearing it at the time, but it's the principle that counts.

So the following day I'm tired. Snoozing through the early evening with no intention going anywhere, when Duncan phones and twists my arm. Next thing I know I'm in the back of a minicab in my second-best vest, feeling a very peculiar sensation indeed. It is heightened by the need to brace myself against the front seat every time the driver brakes. Typical of the cabs round my way, there's no seat belts in the back. As I dig my heels into the rubber mat and try not to tread on his CDs, I have this oddly thrilling sense that *something is about to happen*. To coin a phrase, I feel like I'm going to meet my destiny.

I meet Duncan first, who buys me a beer at the L-shaped bar. He's been out for vodkas in Soho, so he's well-oiled already. I've got catching up to do, but I'm in the mood to do it. It's gone eleven o'clock and the place is filling up. It could be the tubby DJ in his Hawaiian shirt, or the parlour palms decked out in their year-round tinsel; maybe it's the aural sunshine of Stock-Aitken-Waterman floor-fillers beating down from the speakers; whatever the reason, I'm shining too, with a confidence I can usually only muster when I'm on holiday. Nights out at Wallops usually come with too much baggage, and more eyes to avoid than catch.

But tonight – tonight it feels just right.

Plenty of the regular crowd are in for their cheesy-disco fix. This is not a place for your hipper clubbers. They're mostly Outer Londoners coming in: Croydon hairdressers and Bromley diesel dykes; lambswool-jumper queens drinking gin, all of them dipping a toe in the tepid shore of the city scene. It doesn't take many to fill the place. Wallops is as bijou as you'd expect a club under a chip shop to be. Just a bar, a dance floor, loos and a plinth for the DJ. And at one side there are tables with stools where, if you get in quick, you can admire yourself between the facing mirrors into infinity.

Anthony wasn't there when I arrived and I didn't see him come in. That was odd for a start, because Duncan and I are in our usual spot at the end of the bar, with an excellent view of the stairs. We've got our drinks and we're watching everyone come down, grunting and nudging each other appreciatively like stock farmers at an auction.

And then he's here, out of nowhere. Blue jeans, black T-shirt, dark hair. My lager can freezes en route to my lips as he starts to dance. I am Olivia Newton-John, spotting John Travolta on the first day of term at Rydell High. Same jaw hanging open, same spasming crotch. There's an innate sexiness in the way he moves; assured and rhythmically masculine. He looks like that rarest of beasts – a straight man who can really dance. He stands out like foie gras in a burger van, and the pack has caught his scent. Everyone's looking his way. All except Duncan, who's busy assessing a moody hunk by the fire extinguisher. Eventually even he follows my gaze.

'Oh – spunky …' he appraises supportively, though I know he's not his type. But he is exactly mine, from his arrogant swagger to his firm, chunky arse. He's the kind of man I can't resist lusting over in glossy lifestyle magazines, running up beaches with his nuclear family. Or on telly, ordering bitter in pubs or digging up people's gardens. Sometimes he's in supermarkets and often he's on planes, usually seated in business class when I shuffle through to economy.

But tonight he is in Wallops. And I seize the opportunity with a directness that is most unlike me. Had I a sleeve and a fireplace, I'd wipe my mouth on one and throw my scrunched-up beer can in the other. As it is, there's nothing for it but to go and dance beside him. Not *with* him, obviously; in these situations it is apparent indifference, not puppy-dog enthusiasm, that winneth fair gentleman.

His moves are fluid. He dances like a pro. His legs and arms are wired to the beat, his lips to the lyrics of Bananarama. Sensing kinship, I sing mutely from the same song sheet and throw in a few moves of my own. It can only be the beer, but they're coming off pretty well. Two or three other guys have invaded his airspace and are trying to catch his eye. Christmas has come early at Wallops this year and everyone wants to pull the cracker. The man himself is unaware, or so it seems – looking without seeing. His feet may be in South London, on a Perspex floor with integral rope lights, but his head is on the lead float at Sydney Mardi Gras.

The tricky bit is drawing him back.

I try a dance-floor tactic I've had rebuffed a hundred times: a casual jog against his hip followed by an elbow in the back. The others are trying their own variations. It's the kind of personal-space invasion that earns you a beer shampoo in some clubs; here, it's the highest compliment.

From behind the double decks the DJ segues into an Abba megamix. I wonder if he's about to leave the dance floor, and how to avoid getting killed in the rush if he does. But like the music, he doesn't miss a beat ... And in a blink, we're face to face and nose to nose – lip-synching to 'Voulez-Vous', giving it the full Agnetha-and-Frida, like bathroom-mirror karaoke minus the roll-on microphones.

Gotcha.

In the glitter ball's rolling sparkle his eyes are the blue of pre-shrunk denim. My cool kicks in for once: I stifle the urge to turn and check that it's me he's looking at. He smiles. His breath smells of chewing gum and Spanish lager. And he has lovely, lovely teeth. I feel the warmth of his proximity, as keenly as the hatred radiating from the also-rans around us; which I bounce right back at them, off the gleaming shield of my triumph ... *Back to the clawing board, boys – I'm the one that he wants!*

With merciless irony, the Abba megamix slips into 'Gimme Gimme Gimme (A Man After Midnight)', a favourite of mine in any circumstance. But tonight, the occasion and the tempo bring me out in a jubilant strut – and from the edge of the dance floor I catch a warning look from Duncan. It says: 'Act like a nellie now and you've blown it.'

He's right. I keep my arms down.

Then we're looking into each other's eyes and smiling. We still haven't spoken and I'm almost afraid to break the spell ... Till he says, 'What's your name and what's your poison?' – and neither of us vanishes.

'Dan,' I say. 'I'm on Fosters. What's yours?'

''Allo, Dan,' he says, with a cheeky-chappy twang. 'I'm Anthony, and I'll have a bottle of Sol – thanks very much!'

We're still smirking at his verbal dexterity as he steers me to the bar. I buy us both a drink. I feel like a schmuck because I owe Duncan one too, but it doesn't do to invite distraction when you're working on a winner. Then I see him over Anthony's well-delineated shoulder. He has zeroed in on the grumpy hunk, and judging by the smile Dunc's coaxed out of him he'll soon have his hand round a stiff vodka. At the very least.

The pubs have shut by now, so it's getting crowded. Anthony and I fight our way to the seating area. Since the stools are all taken we stand between two tables. It's a snug fit, so wedging ourselves virtually groin-to-groin is, alas, the only option. The more I look at him, the more I think I know him from somewhere – but I can't place it. Anyway, how would you forget a man like this? I skirt the ultimate cliché and ask him if he's been here before.

'About a year ago,' he says. 'You?'

'Yeah, but not for a while,' I lie. 'It's funny, cos you look familiar.'

He's nodding. 'I was thinking the same about you. Or maybe it's just those shapes you were throwing to Bananarama!' He pinches me playfully on a budding love handle.

'Excuse me,' I say, pushing back with the force of a sickly toddler. 'Every one an original!'

He does it again, that square-jawed smile which makes his cheeks pucker adorably. He digs his olive-skinned fingers into my sides, teasing but in a different way. Feigning apathy a moment longer would take a better actor than I am, and a second later we're in a full-on clinch. As the citrus tang of lime from the neck of his beer passes from his lips to mine, his torso feels hard and sleek as a panther …

We finish our drinks and he buys me another, which is a relief. He's brought a smile to my trousers as well as my face, and the fact he isn't insolvent gets another tick. That he might also have a decent job is surely too much to hope for?

'So, what do you do with yourself?' he asks, getting in first. 'Professionally I mean …'

'I'm in advertising. Copywriter. It means I write the—'

'Yeah, I know what it means. I'm in advertising, too … Account director at Radius Direct. But let's not talk about work – I've had a crap week …'

Well, well. I didn't see that coming. Gays in adland are in short supply, even among the creatives. In Account Handling they're rarer still. Anthony, I have no doubt, looks cute in a suit... How extremely well this is turning out, I think, as I put down my lager and kiss him again.

In the mirror, I see one of my dance-floor rivals gazing icily at the back of my head. And beyond, on the other wall, I see myself and one of Anthony's eyes where his head is tilted over. I'm pleased to see it is closed in concentration, instead of looking around like mine.

And that's the moment I realise I was right: tonight was meant to happen.

That feeling in the taxi makes perfect sense now, because this is the beginning of something. Rather than the beginning *and* the end, like the traffic warden last night ... Phone numbers will be exchanged; passions will be replayed. On the scantest of evidence, I already know that here is a man worthy of me; the hungry eyes turned in our direction confirm it ... I, Dan, have waited a long, long time for someone like this – but now he's here, and soon he will feel the same about me.

Between the dry ice and the cigarette smoke there is barely room to breathe. I need to get him out of here, away from the predatory hordes. Get him home, to where the night is quiet and the air is clear. To where we have only each other, and no need of a subtle arrangement of mirrors to admire each other infinitely.

CHAPTER FOURTEEN

It's another sunny morning for the brazenly lazy. I'm at my laptop, all set for my fix of click4dick, when I cast an eye over the shouty news headlines parading across the screen uninvited. It is only as I read the journalistic flag-waving about Tim Henman's chances at Wimbledon that I realise it's June – and Sandra and I still haven't had that conversation about the future.

I hope the fact she hasn't been in touch means she's slipped into leisure mode as easily as I have. Except, that's not Sandra. My ex-art director's batteries are self-charging; she is pathologically incapable of sitting still for five minutes. Her idea of relaxation is a marathon aerobics weekend.

When the axe fell she would have done her sums, same as I did. But once she factored in the school fees and other kiddie costs, her answers will have been starkly different. I know she wouldn't go looking for work without telling me, but she must be up to something. Up to now I've been having too much fun to care, but I am a little curious.

There's no reply at her home. I leave a message, though that's no guarantee; their answerphone has been playing up since it went in with the terrapins. When I call again I leave a message with Lizzie, the middle one. That's not infallible either; Lizzie has a memory like a sieve, plus she's playing a computer game so I have less than her full attention.

Third time, Sandra answers. It's been six weeks since

we lost our jobs and she sounds okay, if a bit nervous. She's glad I called, she says; wants to meet for a chat. I'm about to suggest somewhere new in town, till I remember the havoc dyslexia plays with her sense of direction. We arrange to meet at New York Fitness tomorrow, and go for a bite to eat from there.

I want to do a workout first, so I arrive at quarter past eleven – a quiet time of day. There's no sign of Sandra in the gym, which probably means she's in the Pilates class, frightening girls half her age with her awesome bendiness.

I love the gym when it's like this. No queuing for machines, no distracting eye candy. Just me and the old guy with a ponytail who's always on the sit-up mats. Personal trainers wander around with their clipboards and rationed smiles. Two of them, East European girls in blue mascara, are doing quadricep stretches on static treadmills. As they chat away on one leg I flirt with the idea of hitting Quick-Start, just for the hell of it.

Six sets for chest, six sets for shoulders … A quick shower, and I'm waiting for Sandra outside the changing rooms. She emerges from the door marked with a silhouette like Darcey Bussell after a vicious bout of food poisoning. As always she is festooned with bags and holdalls. She's winding her customary ribbons into her damp hair as she stands on tiptoe to kiss me.

'How are you – all right?' she chirps.

Hugging her is like hugging a twelve-year-old. As I lift her clean off the ground, her perfume transports me back to the office. Only now its scent is pure, unsullied by the top notes of spray glue and Magic Marker.

The receptionist is distracted as we pass through on the way out. So we ignore the 'Please Take One' sign, scooping up handfuls of the promotional KitKats left there unsportingly by the management. We look at each other guiltily, but it's for the calories, not the purloining.

'Mine are for the kids!' she digs as we climb the stairs. 'What's your excuse?'

Outside, she grabs my arm as we cross the zebra. Sand has never mastered traffic.

'I booked us a table at Mosaics,' I say, heading up Buckingham Palace Road.

I'm hungry now, and they do a good line in burgers for me and salads for her. We've got a table in the upstairs alcove, with a carnation in a sherry schooner and a view of the day's specials. Sandra and I have been here loads of times, usually for a quiet powwow when Lionel was winding us up. It's a nice little place, handy for Chartwell Shanks but well off the agency's social radar. We were careful to keep it that way.

'So, how's it going?' she asks. 'And how are The Boys?'

We have some catching up to do, so I order a bottle of wine. I fill her in on the stormy demise of Jack and Phil, plus a few extra details of my private life fine-tuned for her heterosexual ears. Sandra listens with rapt attention as she pulls items of jewellery from her bag. These are her trademark trappings, shed for the gym. A minute later, her every finger and lobe is re-encrusted with something sparkly.

By the time we get round to talking about work, I'm on my second glass and she's on her third menthol fag. I don't know if she's skirting the issue, but I am. From the cursory scan I've given the vacancies section of *Agency Age* in the newsagents, there are more jobs for teams than solo art directors. Which means if Sandra wants a job, she's got more chance if I look with her.

Cue a potentially friendship-straining choice: do I deny myself the rest of this blissfully torpid summer; or do I fritter it away with her underfed, underfunded children on my conscience?

'Well …' I say, as the waitress delivers a bowl of olives.

'Well,' says Sandra. 'What have you decided?'

She's looking straight at me but her eyes are impossible to read. I've a suspicion she's being very British, preparing herself for the worst. I wish I could stomach olives, because I've nothing else to put off the moment.

'Sand – I don't want to go back to work yet. This might be the only chance I ever get to take a sabbatical. I know it's probably not what you want to hear, but I've decided to take the rest of the summer off. Think about work after my birthday … Sorry. I hope you can understand.'

There, I've said it.

Sandra leans back and closes her eyes. Exhales a minty, double-barrelled stream of smoke in silence.

'I am so fucking glad you said that!' She smiles, crouching over the table in a gesture animal behaviourists would interpret as relief. 'I didn't know how I was gonna break it to you! I've enrolled in a summer-school course – Twentieth-Century History. I was dreading telling you, in case …'

The rest of the meal is a celebration. Bacon cheeseburger and fries for me, prawn salad for her, sticky toffee pud to share. All washed down with another cheeky bottle of house white.

'… I was picking up Lizzie from judo the first week,' she explains, forking up a prawn. 'And I heard this other mum talking about the local college. How she'd signed up for a course in – oh, what's that massage thing? – sounds like shit …'

'Shiatsu?'

'That's it. So I asked her what else they do, and she gives us a leaflet. Well, you know how pissed off I get cos I never know anything about the war and politics and that? So I thought, sod it, and signed up. The dole's paying the fees, and Dave's got a bonus at work so we're keeping the au pair on when the schools break up. Sorted!' She raises her glass for another chink. 'Bob's your uncle, Fanny's your aunt!'

I can't believe my luck. The waitress takes our pudding plates and I order us both a calming latte. As usual, I've had two glasses of wine for every one of Sandra's, and as usual she's been talking too much to notice. She can't take her alcohol anyway, but those lippy-tipped butts in the ashtray work out at three per glass, so she's having a good time. She knows she needs to kick the habit, but while she is still setting the treadmill on a gradient that'd leave a gecko begging for crampons, it ain't going to happen. She doesn't smoke in front of her kids – so when she's out, she goes for it.

The more I drink, the more I realise I've missed her. I'm soon engrossed in the latest instalment in the saga of her next-door neighbour. He's a divorced chiropodist with a much younger girlfriend and a weakness for port; it's one of the many soapy strands of life in Morley Road NW10 I've followed for years, when I should have been writing about tax-efficient funeral plans. She's got to the bit about calling the police in the middle of the night when her neighbour shinned up the wrong drainpipe and put his foot through her skylight. And that's when I notice our waitress, wafting the cloths off the other tables and laying fresh ones.

It's gone five-thirty. But Sandra doesn't care. She's on a roll.

'Let's have one more, eh?' she slurs.

Experience has taught me this is inadvisable if she's ever to get home. Putting her on the tube now is out of the question. The only option is to pour her into a taxi and hope the driver doesn't pull up in a dark alley and try on all her jewellery. Which, I guess, means one more won't hurt.

I'm about to order us both a spritzer when Sandra's mobile beeps from the depths of one of her bags. By the time she's liberated it from a sweaty leotard, two free newspapers, half a dozen KitKats, a make-up pouch, a broken Barbie and enough scrunchie hairbands for a team of rhythmic gymnasts, it has long fallen silent. I help her clear everything back off the table as she listens to the message.

'Bollocks – I forget to tell you!' she says, hand flying to her forehead. 'I saw Lalita in Legs, Bums 'n' Tums last week. She said the agency's promoted that slimy git Cranleigh Fosdyke to the board. They're having a do to celebrate and she said we should pop along …'

I know what's coming.

'And, guess what – it's tonight!'

She smiles at me impishly, swaying back and forth in her seat like a naughty little girl.

'Sandra, I—'

'Oh, go on! Be nice to see old Cranleigh …'

I excuse myself and go for a slash in an alcoholic

haze. This is either a bad idea or a *really* bad idea. I know what Sandra's like when she's had too much to drink. The home truths come out to play thick and fast, the way mine did when I was seventeen. What has been a very enjoyable day up to now has the potential to get very messy indeed …

I also remember I've half arranged a date tonight, with a tasty-looking black guy called KEV33. I meant to message him on click4dick this afternoon, not thinking I'd be out this long … There's nothing for it, I decide, steadying myself on the tiles as I wrestle with my fly buttons. I'll just tell her I can't go, then get her into a taxi.

'Thanks, have a nice evening!' calls the waitress as I shuffle back to the table.

'All paid for,' says Sandra, thrusting her arm down the wrong sleeve of her jacket. 'My treat!' She gives up on the jacket and ties it round her waist, then stoops to garland herself with a fluorescent satchel and the holdall with the broken zip. 'Handbag, mobile, check, check … Right, we're all set. Lalita says they're in the Grapes and there's a card behind the bar!'

'Sandra, I really think—'

'And before you start, I know we've been there ten times before. But I still can't remember which pub that is, so you'll have to lead the way.'

That's that, then. I can't leave her on her own. There is no escape.

'*Ta-ta!*' Sandra calls to the waitress, who is trying not to laugh.

I pick up my gym bag and follow her down the stairs.

What the hell … It can't do your career any harm,

getting pissed and lairy with an agency when they've already sacked you.

Can it?

*

The Grapes is the favourite haunt of the engine-room boys at Chartwell Shanks: the Production department and the design studio. Which makes it an odd choice for Cranleigh's celebration piss-up. He's more a chablis-and-canapés man, so the decision smacks of politics.

The agency lot are already there when we arrive. In fact, they practically fill the place. It's a good turnout, though I can't see any sign of the new board director himself. Everyone looks weary, like they've had a hard day at the office. I do my best to look enviably relaxed, but that's easier said than done when you're trying to hold even quite a small woman upright.

Sandra is jubilant and unstoppable. ''Allo, you bunch of bastards!' she calls to the knot of familiar faces at the bar.

'*Sand!*' yells Lalita, clambering down from her stool to give us both a hug. Her ebony bob is newly streaked in electric blue.

'Like the hair, you old tart!' cajoles Sandra as I order us both an orange juice.

I say hi to a couple of guys who seem half-pleased, half-embarrassed to see us. The barmaid is new and takes ages tracking down the juice carton. It's an odd feeling, being back here, waiting for a drink under the same old agricultural implements and prints of Edwardian wine-treaders. The gloom of a working day seems to go with this pub; standing here without it, I feel out of place yet triumphant. Like a militant naturist queuing up at the post office.

Everyone wants to know how I am and what I'm doing. It's hard to explain you're doing-sod-all-and-loving-it without sounding smug. To avoid paying, I ask someone which director's picking up the tab. Surprisingly, it's Lionel Shanks, which can only mean he's here somewhere. Then I spot him; holed up in a corner by the fruit machine with Cranleigh, Astrid Brazier and Stewart, her junior account executive and alleged squeeze.

Lionel's not the sort to frequent a spit-and-sawdust hostelry like the Grapes, any more than Cranleigh. He's huddling for comfort with his mates and a glass of red, and looks distinctly ill at ease. I should go and pay my respects, since technically I'm enjoying his largesse under false pretences. But before I can weave my way over, Lionel's expression grows bleak; Sandra has spotted him, and she's got that dangerous look.

She staggers over with a large glass of someone else's wine, dragging her feet like a trucker in cha-cha heels.

''Allo you lot. How's it going?'

'Sandra, how are you, old girl?' says Cranleigh, standing dutifully to embrace her with the hint of a wobble. He sweeps a hand through his fulsome locks, which is unnecessary; the amount of hair mousse he uses would keep a yeti neat in a high wind.

Sandra eschews his cheek and plants a smacker on his forehead. Lionel and the others look startled. Cranleigh offers her a stool by lifting off his corduroy jacket, which is folded inside-out to protect it from the smoky fug. She ignores him and plops herself down between Lionel and hunky Stewart.

'Fancy meeting you here,' says Lionel, with a quaver.

'How *are* you, Sandra?' asks Astrid, with woman-to-womanly earnestness.

'I'm pissed as a brewer's arsehole, Astrid; how are you?'

Stewart laughs, but the rest of them fall silent. Their discomfort is palpable. They look like the top table at a wedding when the speeches turn blue.

I can't watch, so I go and find Lalita. I'm still holding the other orange juice, so I tip it into her vodka.

'Ta, doll,' she says. 'Sand off the leash tonight, then?'

'Only a lot.'

Sandra's party antics are the stuff of legend. Like the time she ended up face-down on a pool table, trying to blow a sausage roll into the corner pocket. I round up her holdalls, which are by the door where she dropped them. As usual, they are gaping, exposing her knick-knacks to the world. She regularly gets her purse pinched on these occasions but she never, ever learns.

'It's dead boring without you two,' says Lalita. 'I still look for you when I pass your office. It's all stacked up with PCs now, since the upgrade.' She spits an ice cube into her glass. 'Sad …'

That there isn't a new team sitting at our desks makes me feel slightly less dispensable. We chat a while longer, then I do the rounds for a bit, catching up with people I like. Two more secretaries, girly mates of Lalita's, come over and give me a squeeze. Everyone is surprised to see us; you'd think we'd been buried, not fired. It's like being back from the dead, or whatever carpet the memories of surplus colleagues get swept under.

I grill the seccies for office gossip, but it is disappointingly sparse. Denzil's wife is expecting number four; that photocopier engineer I had the hots for is dating Lalita's sister, purely on the strength of a photo jamming up the automatic sort.

'What's Sandra doing now?' asks one of the girls, craning over my shoulder.

I look round. She is sprawled across Stewart's well-constructed lap, much to Astrid's distaste. His sleeves are rolled up over his smooth, fly-half's forearms as he attempts to light the fag clamped between Sandra's lips. Against my better judgement, I zero in.

'Dan,' says Lionel, with his best approximation of a smile. 'How very nice to see you. Both.'

Whenever Lionel smiles, one incisor catches vampirically on his lower lip. I ask how's business; a question he fields like it's a trick and like he thinks I give a shit. I offer to get the drinks in, courtesy of his expense account, but he won't hear of it.

'Allow me,' he says, hopping up as if scalded. 'What's yours, Dan? And what about, er … ?'

Sandra is giggling and playing with Stewart's tie. They are whispering away.

'I'll have a bottle of Bud, thanks, Lionel. And something soft for Sandra.'

Her ears prick up at this.

'Eh?!' she squawks. 'You can keep it if it's soft – it's no bloody use to me!' She throws back her head and lets loose a smoky cackle, almost losing her perch.

'Steady!' says Stewart. His voice has a deep and beery Home Counties charm. 'Don't want to lose you again, do we …'

Astrid shoots him a glacial glare. I try to think of something to deflect her attention, but she snaps up her Burberry purse/organiser and makes for the ladies. I sit and keep her seat warm, smiling weakly at Cranleigh who, according to the girls, has been on the piss since lunchtime.

'Congrats on the promotion,' I say. 'You still doing a three-day week?'

Cranleigh is glassy-eyed. His chin bobs slightly, as if on a gentle sea. We appear to be experiencing some sort of delay. It's a full five seconds before he can fix me in focus. He replies in a sort of verbal Morse code.

'Thanks … Old man. Dunno … Hope so. Trains … Bastards …'

This is presumably reference to his commute from the family seat in the Peak District. Thanks to an MP-style pied-à-terre in Kennington, it is a journey Cranleigh endures only a couple of times a week. To hear him sound off about it, you'd think he was riding the Burma Railway in a leech-filled body bag; heaven forbid his elevation to the board should expose him to the hoi polloi an iron-mile longer.

Cranleigh and I had little enough to say to each other when we worked together, so as he lapses into a middle-distance nirvana we sit in silence … Not for the first time, I watch in wonder as Sandra canoodles with a man barely half her age. It never goes anywhere, but she likes the attention when she gets it. She's still got it at forty-five; good on her, I say.

Lionel can't spin out buying a round any longer. He starts to ferry drinks back from the bar.

'Bud for you, Dan … Another for you, Stew … Large chianti for Cranleigh … Astrid's having a small pinot …'

'I've got Astrid's *pee-no* right 'ere!' pipes up Sandra, squirming in Stewart's lap. 'Dunno 'ow small it is, though …'

Lionel's fang is resting on his lip again.

'And a bitter lemon,' he mumbles, disappearing back to the bar.

I help myself to an open packet of salt-and-vinegar. 'Let me know when you want a taxi, Sand,' I suggest hopefully.

'Oh, don't be such a bleeding killjoy! Stewie's just telling me about his 'amstring. Pulled it doing rugby training – didn't you?'

Stewart nods. 'Squat thrusts.' He's looking me in the eye, that way I wish hot straight men wouldn't when they're talking about their thighs.

Astrid reappears. I give her back the stool. She's the soberest of the lot of us, tightly wound as ever. We've all heard the rumours, but even Lalita and the secs aren't sure what the score is with her and Stewart. If they are getting it on, they've been miraculously discreet.

'What the fuck's this?' says Sandra as Lionel hands her a drink.

I cringe, even though he's no longer our boss, and give her my hardest stare. 'I think you've had enough, Sand. It's—'

She swigs it in a puff of smoke like a witch's potion.

'Uuurgh, bitter lemon! It tastes how you look, Astrid!'

She cackles again and Stewart joins her with a chesty laugh. There's a chemistry between them I've never noticed before. Aside from the day we had a team-drool over his motorcycle leathers, I can't ever remember Sandra paying him much attention. I find myself wondering if they had something going on all the time and I missed it – something fate has reawakened tonight. Except it wasn't fate who frogmarched me to the Grapes, now was it?

I'm getting that warning feeling at the back of my eyes that says I've hit my limit ... And suddenly we're a tableau, captured in time: the six of us, round this table, separate from the hubbub of chatter, the clinking glasses and the tinny gurgle of the fruit machine. Like the closing scene of a touring whodunnit:

– Astrid does not flicker; just looks into her wine in silence;

– Cranleigh stares into space, pale and wide-eyed; if that torn banquette wasn't holding him up, he'd slide to the floor leaving a snail-trail of blood on the wall;

– Lionel is at my shoulder, muttering, lost in his own agenda;

– Sandra and Stewart are on the stool, nuzzling and giggling earthily.

And me, I am the camera. Watching a slice of my life, or rather a slice of my past; where I used to be, what I used to do. Whether I carry on with it is a decision I haven't taken yet. In this moment, everything hangs in the balance.

Stewart catches me looking. 'I resigned today,' he says. 'I'm going to bike across Oz with my mates. Sydney to Perth.' He nods over his shoulder, into the other world at the crowded bar. 'That lot don't know yet.'

Sandra smiles at me approvingly; she knew. She unclasps the beer from Stewart's hand, raises it in a toast and takes a slug.

'Good on yer, mate. And happy landings!'

Then she jumps off his knee and slurs, 'This calls for a *shhh-elebration* ...'

Uh-oh: this looks dangerous. She's casting round for something, hair ribbons fluttering like a maypole. Next thing I know she's down on all fours, searching under the tables.

'KitKats all round when I find my fucking bag … You'll have a finger, won't you, Astrid?'

CHAPTER FIFTEEN

KEV33 blanks me the next time I send him a message. I try again and a box pops up: *SORRY. THIS USER HAS BARRED YOU FROM MESSAGING.*

That's the end of him, then. Drama queen.

I'm not too bothered, nice as he looks in his pictures. Tell you the truth, I've been trying to lay off the brutal shaggery of late. Ever since I calculated how many men I've met since I split with The Boys. It took a lot of sifting through my Filofax and my sent-emails to Duncan, but I got there.

Twenty-six. That's more than three a week. And I dread to think how many hours I spent panning for them. Not that I have to be there as such, nose to screen, fingers to keyboard. Sometimes I'll just hook up to click4dick and let the laptop get on with it ... Go about my business, leaving those hot-man messages to stack up till I can be bothered to check back.

My routine goes like this: *Log on ... Pop to the shops ... Come home ... Check messages ... Unpack groceries and make cup of tea ... Check messages ... Put wash on ... Check messages ... Hunt for CD in cupboard by the laptop ... Check messages ... Sit and bid for something on eBay ... Check messages ... Check email ... Check messages ...*

See, I might as well be on a long piece of elastic.

And the guys themselves – well, they were fine. Mostly. In fact, three or four of them were very fine, and two of those were allegedly single. I meant to do something about them. Meet up again, maybe get to know them a bit. Maybe get to like them.

Maybe even stop all this.

But it's not as easy as that.

The daytime crowd on click4dick is a whole new ballgame. Actually, make that 'sweetshop'. I'm like a kid with the key to a confectioner's, eyes as wide as party plates as he watches the whole yummy stock change throughout the day.

This is getting too difficult because it's getting too easy. Sweeties and sex: you can have too much of both. I feel like a whore and a junkie. And a junkie-whore ... When I look at what else is in my Filofax over the last few weeks, it makes sobering reading. A lunch here, a movie there, but no modern-history lectures for me. No plans fulfilled; no structure to the days. Nothing for my mind at all. I'm entrapped by the possibility of sex, worse than I ever was. When I was working, pre-arranged hook-ups were a nice diversion, like going to the gym only sweatier. But now, in this golden time when I could be doing anything – going anywhere – they're eating my life away.

How did I get like this? In the days when I went to bars, the yen for men was still a game; an added frisson to a fun night out. But now, when I'm home alone, there's no pretending I'm there to chat, have a drink, meet my buddies or dance. This is desire distilled to its very essence, all social trappings evaporated away.

Somewhere down the line, wanting a man and a relationship has mutated into something grotesque. I've sidetracked myself into settling for sex; for banging away at a solitary note instead of playing a tune.

How much longer am I going to be like this? I'm nearly forty, for fuck's sake!

Just to rub it in, there's a card on the mantelpiece. Hand-embossed, with gold edges and swirly type. It's from my Aussie buddy Justin, and Peter his boyfriend of four years. A cordial invitation to their wedding, no less.

Actually, a bit less: it's an invitation to their commitment ceremony. Gays aren't allowed to get married; but, thanks to Ken Livingstone, if you live in London you can now get the registry-office equivalent. The ceremony is next week, at City Hall on the South Bank. The prim white card has been peering at me from behind the clock for a while, and I'm still not sure what to think ... Shameful I know, but I stand aside from all those gay rights' arguments these days. I did my marching when I first came to London, on Gay Pride days and protests against Clause 28. I guess I've grown complacent since then.

Being gay doesn't seem so hard any more. But being gay and not being a hussy – that's tough. I'd still march for that.

*

I quite enjoy looking at flats with Duncan. Partly because it's fun and partly because it makes me feel so damned pleased with myself. I'd no idea how much the value of my place has rocketed – you couldn't get a chicken coop round here for what I paid for it.

I get used to Dunc's enigmatic directions flashing up on my mobile:

CORNER OF ACRE WAY AND
TREGOTHNAN ST 4PM. CAN YOU
BRING MEASURING TAPE.

Or:

GROUND FLOOR 34 LYSIAS AVE. THINK
I MAY HAVE SHAGGED THE GUY
UPSTAIRS.

However he puts it, it means he wants a second opinion. And this particular afternoon we're looking at two properties. I arrive at the first in good time, and I'm standing in the sun by the wheelie bins awaiting further instructions. It's in a road off the high street lined with big imposing terraces, on the cusp of where Clapham North becomes Brixton. Prices here are what estate agents call 'realistic', thanks to an enterprising drug trade and the occasional drive-by shooting.

I spot the fluorescent-green Smart car long before it pulls up at the kerb. It's emblazoned with the logo of Thresholds, a local estate agent, and I can't resist a smile at Duncan's discomfort visible through the windscreen. He unfolds from the plastic passenger seat with a glare that dares me to laugh.

'I'd have brought my car if I knew she had a vitamin pot on wheels,' he says. Dunc's earthy Glaswegian frankness is one of his most endearing qualities.

The estate agent, a breezy girl in her twenties, is rummaging for something in the glove compartment.

'Here we are!' she says. A Thresholds fob with four keys dangles from an immaculately wrapped fingernail. 'Let me feed the meter and I'll be right with you ...'

We wait inside the gate while she finds the right key. The front door snags on the carpet, so she pushes like she's launching a lifeboat. The hall smells of neglect; we step over a confetti of curry-house flyers and buff-coloured bills.

'This is the one,' she says, unlocking another door halfway along. She stands aside as Duncan and I troop down the stairs.

'Did you know it was a basement flat?' I whisper as he inspects the lounge.

'It's lower ground floor *and* upper ground floor,' chirps the estate agent before he can answer. 'Bedroom's up there.'

She points to a spiral staircase, half-obscured by IKEA units.

It's not as gloomy as I expected, at least with the sun shining. Legs and pushchairs pass by through the top half of the security-grilled window. It's like the view from a lift when the doors open between floors.

I'm trying my best to see the flat and not the furnishings, but it's hard to overlook a canoe. It is eight feet long, lying upside down under the window ... Now, who would live in a flat like this? The shelf units also smack of hearty outdoor pursuits, with books about camel trekking and surviving the outback. There's a video of something to do with triathletes which, judging by the cover, looks right up my alley.

I follow Duncan into the kitchen, where the greasy work surface has 'straight man' written all over it. Further proof is in the fridge magnet of a topless blonde, and the tiny Scrabble tiles underneath that spell out LISA OPENS BEERS THE BANGKOK WAY.

The estate agent is unlocking the back door. 'And if you'd like to see the patio ...'

Outside, there is nothing in the small quadrangle of yard but a blackened barbecue and a mountain bike. The latter is heavily padlocked, which seems overcautious since there's no exit from here. With the high wall topped with chicken-wire, I'd say it's pretty safe from anyone, barring a light-fingered abseiler living upstairs.

'Room for a canoe out here, if you ask me,' says Duncan, reading my mind. He's as house-proud as I am.

I can tell from his tone he's not sold, but it's still worth a gander up the spiral staircase. The one bedroom has a whiff of trainers, and tired-looking bedding you wouldn't want to pull back. There are uncapped aerosols on the chest of drawers and a magazine about digital photography; from behind the wardrobe, the tip of a snowboard peeps like a nervous attempt at hide and seek.

'Nice and sunny in the mornings,' says the girl, leaning a hip on the door frame. The upper torso of a stately old black gentleman goes past the bedroom window, as if the Masai have made it to Clapham. It feels odd, to walk upstairs and only be this far off the ground.

There's something a bit sexy about a sporty man's bedroom when he doesn't know you're there, even when it's smelly like this one. I really want to look under the bed.

'Which do you think is his knicker drawer?' whispers Duncan as our tour guide heads to the bathroom.

Is it any wonder we hit it off?

*

The second property is in Waverley Mews, on the other side of Sainsbury's. I can walk it in the time it takes them to negotiate the one-way and park. Which is lucky, because the Smart car's jump seat isn't made for anyone bigger than a Border terrier.

Waverley Mews is a gated development, converted from what the estate agent's spec calls 'Artisans Workshops'. It looks more like a converted car showroom to me, but it has a certain charm. Number five is a studio flat: one big room for living, sleeping and cooking. The ceiling must be twenty feet high, the walls are neatly whitewashed, and the floors the original parquet with no trace of engine oil. It also boasts a cast-iron fireplace ('Original Feature!') and a swanky-looking kitchenette in the corner (Not).

'Where's the bed?' asks Duncan.

The estate agent just smiles and turns up a talon. We're standing right under it.

'Oh,' he says, intrigued. 'But how do you ...'

With the elegance of a magician's accomplice, she slides a concealed ladder from its sheath in the wall.

'That's a relief,' he says. 'I was thinking a trampoline.'

She pushes the ladder into place, clicks the safety catch and invites us to: 'Jump up and have a look!'

The bed is on a gallery, suspended from the ceiling. Duncan hops up like a squirrel. I'm in two minds about following, on grounds of health and safety. But it's a double bed, so presumably built for two; plus there are wellies behind the door that are size eleven at least.

From up here the place has a light, airy feel, with big windows at the front running from eye level up to the ceiling. The bottom panes are frosted, but over the top I can see into the mews forecourt with its communal lawn. And the Smart car, standing obediently in the sunshine, glowing like a sucked lime sherbet.

'I quite like it,' says Duncan, shuffling around on the duvet and looking up at the joists. 'Seems solid enough ...'

I'm first down. I look at the bathroom, which is nearly new like everywhere else, and more savoury than the last one. There's no bath, just a walk-in shower of translucent glass bricks, with a big flat shower head that looks the business. And there's an Indian carving over the bathroom door, similar to the ones above the settee.

In fact, now I look, there are Indian touches everywhere, like the fabric swathed across a teak screen that diverts your eye from the kitchen area. A coffee-table book of Bollywood posters stands face-out from a bookshelf, and on the window sill is a bronze, many-armed god like the one that sprouts swords in *Jason and the Argonauts*.

'Nice property, isn't it?' says the estate agent, sensing Duncan's interest. 'Bit smaller, of course, but you've got the security here, plus the off-street parking. And it's so handy for the tube.'

'And not so handy for the Barrel & Tap, thank God,' whispers Duncan. 'If I bought the other one, I'd never be out of there.'

He's right. Sporty Boy's pad was an enticing stagger from the local pulling parlour. I'm struggling with the latch on a pair of louvre doors, so he gives me a hand.

'What's in here?' he asks the girl.

She flicks to the second page of her notes. 'Erm ... Might be the airing cupboard. Can you manage?'

The latch yields to a hairy Scottish wrist. Behind the doors is a built-in closet the size of a double phone box. His 'n' hers clothes rails run either side of a full-length mirror.

'Oh!' says Duncan. 'I've always fancied a walk-in wardrobe. Look, there's even a thing to put shoes in!'

On the 'his' rail, navy-blue suits are ranked one behind the other, some still in dry-cleaner's covers. Then I notice the hook behind the door.

'Anyway, the spiral staircase in that other place would drive me mad,' he witters. 'If I was him, I'd put a fireman's pole in – think how much fun that'd be … You could have one here too, for getting down from the bed … Be a bugger to shin up though, wouldn't it? … Dan? Are you listening to me?'

On the hook behind the door is a denim jacket; rusty red, the colour of a nosebleed. It's hanging by a little black chain, riveted to the sheepskin collar. Just seeing it up this close is enough to make my teeth clench.

''Course I am, Dunc. That's why firemen's trousers have rubber sewn on the inside-leg. You're not telling me you've never noticed …'

CHAPTER SIXTEEN

At this time of night, a cab from Wallops back to my place takes fifteen minutes. With one hand on Anthony's chunky square knee, I am congratulating myself all the way home.

We hang our jackets over two kitchen chairs, which instantly look made for the purpose. I'm putting the kettle on for coffee, with a flagrant joke about giving him something hot, when it dawns on me I haven't changed the sheets since the traffic warden ... What the hell. It's one more reason to opt for moody lighting when I eventually get him into the bedroom.

And since we soon establish I'm right out of coffee granules, this takes a little under three minutes.

*

As usual, my bladder wakes me next morning. The empty bottle of nearly-champagne I knock over on the way to the bathroom is presumably to blame. I remember now – popping it with magnanimous aplomb as a caffeine substitute. It's been hanging round in the bottom of my fridge for months, waiting for a brainy gay. I hardly dare wake him, just in case. One dumb word in the light of day could ruin everything.

There's a definite feel of Christmas morning as I slip back into bed beside him. Despite his worn, smoky wrappings all over the floor, Anthony still has the aura of an unopened gift. I prop myself on one elbow and watch him lying there, chin up, noble as a sarcophagus. I want to mould myself to him all over again, but I'm also afraid to touch; of reawakening the reality behind those Venus-flytrap eyelashes. Occasionally he stirs and once he turns to face me, like he heard what I'm thinking.

Later, I try not to appear too delighted when he says he doesn't have to rush off. He seems as keen as I am that we get to know each other – and, weirdly, I have no qualms about leaving him alone in my flat as I skip out for coffee and the Sunday papers. Anthony seems like part of the furniture already.

We dovetail in lots of ways. Literally, as we reach out simultaneously to lace fingers while reading the *Observer*. He looks surprisingly tasty in the kimono-style dressing gown I never wear, which might have been made for him. I try not to think of it as I watch him, immersed in his paper – but he does seem like the perfect dinner-party boyfriend, with his insights on everything from the latest NHS crisis to Geri Halliwell's new hair.

Morning wears lazily into early afternoon, and in an easy rapport we work through the sections of the broadsheet we both prefer. We take time out from world events for coffee, the morning-after sugar rush of chocolate biscuits and some thoroughly engaging sex. But there's something else at work here, too – we both feel it. Something beyond pure physical attraction. It takes guts, but neither of us shirks the responsibility: we are agreed it is possible, that this is More Than Just Another Fling.

This could be Something Big.

A burden of this significance lies heavily on us both. By the time we've showered (separately; I don't trust the seal round my bath) we have reached a further accord, and issued a revised communiqué: we both hope and believe this *may* be Something Big, but obviously it's very early days. And either way, whatever happens, we're going to be Really Good Friends.

Hell, we've only just met! Anthony and I (sounds nice, doesn't it?) have so much to learn about each other, even after fourteen hours; eight of them awake, two of them properly sober. So, in a further show of maturity, we profess a shared sense that there is No Rush To Make A Big Commitment.

Under normal gay circumstances, this thinly disguised slamming of the brakes would spell the end of a budding relationship. But, surprising as it sounds, I am not concerned. Deliciously, box-tickingly impressive as Anthony is, there is something about him that makes me uneasy. For I have been here before. I've known men as cute as this, nearly, who were all over me like fake tan and about as long-lasting. Men who swore devotion and made me feel precious; who said they hadn't felt like this in years. Men who held my hand and looked me in the eye as we made plans for the summer after next.

They're the same ones who stopped taking my calls, and evaporated into the ether without a shred of explanation. If I've learned one thing in my life, it is that you can never be sure of anyone. I pride myself there is not a man alive who can shock me with his dastardliness now. Because whatever they do, whatever they say, I'm ready.

I loan Anthony some underwear – sexy but second-division. As he is pulling on his jeans, I say, 'Fancy going for Sunday lunch?'

I regret it immediately. He'll sense that I am too keen, even though we've made it clear we're both cooling off equally. So when he says, 'Yeah, that'd be great,' it's a surprise.

The Frog & Fir Cone serves the best roast beef and Yorkshire pud in Clapham, and it's just across the Common. The day is warm, but Anthony brings his jacket, which I take to mean he isn't coming back to the flat. It is red denim with a detachable sheepskin collar, the 'must-have' item from last winter. They were everywhere, and I nearly bought one myself.

He swings it over his shoulder as we walk. Beer bottles dot the grass, remnants of someone else's Saturday night. From our in-depth chat, I've already established that he's a Beckenham boy, back living with his mum temporarily. But he can also tell me things I never knew about my own neighbourhood.

'See those two mansion blocks? In Queen Victoria's time, they were the tallest buildings in South London. She complained, cos she said they spoiled her view from the Palace.'

'Yeah?' I'm impressed. The monolithic stone terraces on the edge of the Common are favourites of mine. 'How come you know so much about Clapham?'

'I used to live here with my ex,' says Anthony. 'Over on West Side. He was big on local history. Always telling me stuff like that as we walked the dogs.'

'Oh, okay ... He's the one who owned the restaurant in Dulwich, right?'

'Yeah – bastard. We split up in January after four and a half years. Hence me living at my mum's ...'

The sun is shining. The chimneys of Battersea Power Station are four-square on the skyline, like the upturned legs of a dead art deco cow; and, fittingly, I can as good as smell my Sunday roast.

'Anyway, enough about me,' he says. 'I still don't know where you work yet, Mister Copywriter ...'

This gets another tick; I like a man who doesn't just talk about himself. Time to earn a brownie point of my own ...

'Well, you said you'd had a crap week, so I didn't want to talk about it. I'm at Javelin – in Soho Square, you probably know them. They do the same sort of stuff as Radius Direct. That's where you said you are, right?'

I'm suddenly aware I am talking to myself. I turn back to see him standing there, dead in his tracks. If we weren't on an acre of sunny, yellowing sward, I'd swear he was caught in somebody's headlights.

'Anthony ... ?'

And that was when it clicked.

'Fuck me! *Tony, it's you!*'

CHAPTER SEVENTEEN

What do you wear to a gay wedding? I feel I ought to know. Gina obviously thinks I do, judging by her emails since she accepted my invitation to come with.

Duncan is doing an extra Saturday shift at the hospital, so she was my very first second choice. The gold-trimmed card says '& Guest', and although Gina doesn't know Justin and Peter that well, I knew she'd be game, at least from an anthropological point of view. Whether it is white-water rafting or something first-run-and-fringy about paedophiles, she is always up for a new experience.

As usual, I've left it too late to get ready. I'm re-buttoning my favourite shirt as she pulls in at the kerb. I wave down and catch her eye. Gina hates being kept waiting, which means she inadvertently chooses my outfit for me. This shirt, those trousers, that waistcoat will do fine. I leave everything else where it is and slip a tie in my pocket. I only own three, not counting the kosher-dickie I can't tie without the internet; that leaves the idiot-dickie, a slightly too wide silk number with bananas and cherries which would be asking for quips today, and the black tie I bought to bury my gran. That was five years ago, and, like her, it's not seen daylight since.

I grab my sunglasses, invitation and appropriately wrapped gift, slamming the front door behind me.

'No tie?' says Gina as I hop in beside her.

'In reserve,' I say, kissing her on both cheeks. 'I want to see what everyone else is wearing first.'

Gina has opted for chic fawn trousers and a long-sleeved silk blouse.

'No hat?' I niggle as we pull into the main road.

'On your bike.' She is not a hat person. 'Or you can walk – it's a nice day ...'

Gina and I go back years. We worked together at Centaur Publishing in the South Kensington of the late 1980s. She was an editorial assistant; I was bashing out cover blurbs, for everything from Regency bodice-rippers to non-fiction gems like *Nostradamus For Your Dog.* We were drawn together by the fact neither of us fitted the Centaur mould. Publishing in the eighties was populated by immaculate lady lunchers who didn't need the money ('darling') so there was little incentive to pay anyone who did. I had some good times at Centaur; it was my first chance to write and get paid for it. But you had to be at the top of the tree to make decent money, and humble blurb writers dangled from the lower branches.

So, at one of the boozy dos or unfeasibly long lunches on which publishing thrived, Gina and I both admitted our heart wasn't in it. We couldn't take seriously a world where game-show hostesses were courted to write yoga manuals, then revered as a literary powerhouse if they sold a few thousand copies. Figures which, in reality, came down to Centaur's hard-boiled sales reps – or 'the rep-tiles', as they were unaffectionately known in South Ken. Based in Basingstoke, they were the publisher's unsung heroes, ploughing up and down untolled motorways, delivering profits from the back of a company hatchback. I soon learned to spot the reps' cars in the car park, stuffed with sales presenters, well-chewed toys of children they rarely saw, and a nylon hanging wardrobe.

Reps wore signet rings and tinted glasses, and everything about them said Basingstoke. They gloried in chauvinism; so, as the office gay boy, I gave them a wide berth, unlike the blow-dried ladies of Centaur Editorial. The latter tittered in their presence in contrast to what they said about them behind their backs, then tried to screw them at the Christmas party.

Gina was brighter than me. She'd read a lot of the heftier titles on the Centaur list, and it was expected that I would too. Despite my pretensions to be a writer, I made it my mission to read as few books as possible, preferring to crib my blurb from the hardback rather than write my own from scratch. In fact, I remember reading only one from cover to cover. It was the latest shopping-and-fucking epic from Gloria Stark, queen of glitzy Hollywood sleaze. Her novels had been the staple reading of package holidaymakers since the days when Mr Heath was in Number Ten. Even Ted was rumoured to keep one by the bailing scoops aboard Morning Cloud. Either way, like many kids of my generation, I had largely gleaned the facts of life the Beverly Hills exposé way. My older brother had a Gloria Stark on his bookshelf when I was eleven. I used to sneak in and reread pages 131 to 134 – the infamous newts-in-the-jacuzzi scene. A boy in my class could recite the dirty bits word for word, which caused no end of mirth when the axolotl came up in biology.

I trundled through the job without straining myself unduly. Until, like Gina, I decided my future did not lie among the big-haired Sloanes and frascati launches of publishing. We jumped ship about the same time; me into advertising, where salaries were better and no one pretended it was art; her to the National Theatre, on the

South Bank of the Thames. She has been there ever since, which has been great for me because she gets two freebies for every show. And great for her because, as a single girl, the female bias of publishing was a bore, and here at least there were men. Except, backstage to box office, they were mostly gay – so great for me again.

We crawl into central London through the weekend traffic. Congestion charging, another of Mayor Livingstone's innovations, only applies in the week so the traffic is seething. To make matters worse, the lights are out at Vauxhall. Gina snaps down her visor and hunts for something funky on the radio.

'It's been like this all bloody week!'

Gina likes her car. A free parking space at the National comes with the job, which is dead handy for today. We're still in good time, and even dusty Waterloo looks inviting in the sunshine ... A converted fire station is now a trendy bar, its giant doors thrown open to the air. It's only 10.30 a.m., but there's already a crowd. A chalkboard on the pavement announces ENGLAND V. AUSTRALIA – LIVE BY SATELLITE. Punters in rugby shirts and clam diggers eat fried breakfast before a giant screen. It's going to hit eighty-five degrees, according to the weatherman. I direct a stream of fetid air from the dashboard into my face.

'Won't be just the bridegrooms glowing at this rate,' I say, wriggling out of my waistcoat and tossing it in the back.

'Which one's wearing white?' asks Gina innocently.

'Cheeky. Apparently it's matching navy lounge suits.'

'Huh. That's as close as Justin will get to the navy ...'

She has only met him and Peter once: my Eurovision

131

Song Contest party, a couple of years ago. Justin is a successful account man in adland, though you'd never have guessed it that night. Not in the Cher glitter wig. He's from Darwin originally; the way he tells it, from borderline Ocker stock, with one or two nefarious relatives he was more than happy to escape by moving to London. Justin was always a bit of a wild one. Till he met Peter, who's done him nothing but good.

We arrive at the National Theatre, home of envelope-pushing drama disguised as a multi-storey car park. Gina flashes her pass at the barrier and drives down into the part of the building where form best suits function. We take the lift and emerge in the theatre foyer. She's striding out like a hockey mistress.

'I don't want to see the house manager,' she hisses, eyes to the floor. 'He's been after me all week about the seats I got mother for the Berkoff …'

A platform recital is going on beside the bookshop; an ensemble in green-felt tunics, tootling on medieval instruments for an earnest audience of six.

'Hey nonny, nonny,' she says. We make a beeline for the exit.

Outside, the riverside promenade is packed with every race and creed. Families on their way to the aquarium; backpackers posing for pictures on the wall. The Thames looks brown and murky as we follow the walkway to Blackfriars Bridge. In Gina's time here, the South Bank has transformed from a badland of warehouses to an urban playground, with shops, restaurants and gallerias all thirsting for a river view.

It's an easy walk to City Hall. We chat about her work on the way, plus any passing blokes worth dissecting. Tate Modern we pass without a word. It is the scene of the only row we've ever had, on a day as hot as this last year when the escalators failed. I lost my cool after one too many Emins and a video installation of harlequins leaping about in offal; Gina, more culturally resilient than I am, wanted to see the rest – so there, like our opinions, we diverged.

I shift my wedding present to the other arm. We reach the Millennium Bridge, extending across the river from the dome of St Paul's Cathedral like the tongue of a chameleon. For architectural charm, you can't beat a wooden footbridge: the Pont des Arts in Paris, Charles Bridge in Prague ... This one is steel but it isn't bad, even if it has ruined a classic *Doctor Who* location. On my teenage bedroom wall I had a poster of the Cybermen, marching inexorably down the stone steps of St Paul's on one of their regular, interplanetary invasions of the Home Counties. Said steps were, alas, obliterated when this bridge was built. But if the silver marauders from Mondas ever return, they at least have a direct route to Tate Modern without rusting their blasters.

Rugby jerseys in white or gold appear on the promenade. England have won, judging by the jubilant high-fives and a passing chorus of 'Swing Low, Sweet Chariot'. More than a few wearers are staggering slightly; in the sunshine, some have shucked off their jerseys altogether. Gina is quite amenable to this. She likes rugby and, unlike me, knows one end of the pitch from the other. She could do with a rugger bugger of her own, in my opinion ... Gina is a bit chronically single, for no good reason I can see. She is as smart as she is elegant: a catch, where other girls are but tinny, sparkling lures on the end of a line.

Past HMS Belfast, City Hall comes into view, like a domino beehive caught in the act of toppling. It's only been open a year or two. Big and shiny, more glassy than classy, but it makes an impact. If I'm honest, I'm as interested in having a snoop inside as seeing the ceremony itself. Justin and Peter are great, but I'm a bit dubious about this whole partnership thing. I'm on the old-fashioned side of gay sensibility; the one that says, if straight people want to get married or lie in a foxhole facing enemy artillery without us, that's fine by me.

The Hall has an appropriately Saturday feel. I can see one or two people inside, though the doors are locked until we buzz.

'Who are you here for?' asks Security, armed with a walkie talkie. I hold out the invitation to him. 'Justin and Peter … Over there, please.'

There are a few ceremonies scheduled for this morning. Knots of uncertain-looking spectators gather at points on the building's circumference; our group numbers about a dozen. No sign of the guys themselves; in fact I don't recognise anyone. I smile at one or two gingers, who have to be relatives of Peter even if they are a foot shorter. They also have a purer Irish twang, which implies they've come over specially. All the women have had their hair done, aunts and nieces sharing the same style: razored at the neck, firmly pomaded, like they just took off a crash helmet.

'Do we expect a big entrance?' asks Gina. 'Pardon the expression ...'

'I don't know, but they'd better get a shift on. It's half-eleven – they're on in quarter of an hour.'

At that moment, the lift doors open and a freshly processed party descends the ramp. The couple, clearly both happy and gay, are women in their mid-thirties. They smile, clutching red and white bouquets that match their outfits as they scamper outdoors hand in hand. The rest of their party follows: a mix of the inescapably gay, the comfortably straight and the strait-laced but dutiful. The newlyweds themselves are setting up a bouquet-toss, when I spot Justin and Peter heading across the terrace. With them are their friends Nigel and Amelie, who have official roles as best man and best woman. All of them carry take-out coffees the size of beach buckets. Peter looks relaxed, winking to us as he walks in; Justin looks focused, if apprehensive.

'We were early so we went to Starbucks,' he tells a woman in a jade-green dress. I smile when he looks my way, just as a girl calls out, 'Justin and Peter – *now, please!*' and waves us to the lifts.

'Tie!' says Gina as we ascend to the top floor.

We are shown into a functional function room with rows of chairs and a lectern. An efficient-looking man in a suit is changing the discs on a CD player. The bridal party disappears so Gina and I take a pew halfway back, stowing our wedding gift under the seat. The view from here is amazing: London, stretching south for miles in a monochrome nightmare; acres of austere concrete, broken up by patches of green and one or two noble spires. I'm surprised at the noise up so high – a helicopter and the distant rumble of rolling stock. But my musing is curtailed by a blast of Ennio Morricone as Justin and Peter troop out from behind a screen, each with their best person for support.

Peter, reputedly the country's third-youngest headmaster, looks relaxed as he strides to the front. He gives us all eye contact, and a smile of both excitement and relief. Justin, marketing guru of this parish, looks rigid with fear; he can barely co-ordinate smile and legs at once, while Amelie, his childhood friend from Darwin, beams from under standard-lamp sized headgear.

I've never seen him so nervous. He edges forward as Nigel and Amelie withdraw, leaving him and Peter standing side by side by Hugo Boss. The music ends, and the registrar launches into an opening address. It's about the importance of demonstrating commitment, and sharing the day with friends. All a bit soulless – till we get to the bit on the order sheet called 'Exchange of Vows'. Not the parroted promises I'm expecting, but words the guys have written themselves. They're declarations of what they mean to each other, which I find unexpectedly moving. More so, when a quivering Justin stumbles to a halt with:

'Peter, since the day we met, I …'

There's an awkward moment before the registrar steps in to read the rest for him. And the show goes on. Peter reads his without a hitch. Of the two, he's more accustomed to public speaking, albeit to an audience that are small and sit cross-legged. For a moment the atmosphere is magical. Till he pauses for breath at the line '… all that you mean to me ...' at which point a faraway train parps impolitely.

Gina flinches, but I keep eyes to the front. If that was me up there, I'd now be on the carpet.

Amelie and Nigel nip forward with matching blue boxes. We watch in respectful silence as Justin and Peter exchange rings, presumably for the first time in public. They adjourn to a table, topped with a vase of fleshy gladioli, and take turns to sign the register.

The registrar closes the proceedings, with thank-yous and a joke about England vs The Wallabies, which goes over more heads than the lesbians' bouquet. There's just time for a photo before we're herded into the lifts. Gina and I crowd in beside the woman in the jade dress; and, as we plunge back to earth, I feel oddly uplifted.

When the bridal party reappears, we head into the sun. I realise I'm still embracing a gift-wrapped picnic service that it's high time I offloaded. I go and give Justin a hug and reintroduce him to Gina. He's leaning on the river wall looking smiley and elated.

'Well done, matey! Were you okay? You looked a bit nervous.'

'Cacking myself!' says Justin. His carefully sculpted fringe bobs over his Versace sunglasses. 'Haven't been that scared since I got caught in a drugs bust when I was eight.' He sparks up a fag. 'This time I hadn't even done anything!'

'Nice vows,' says Gina. 'Very touching.'

'Cheers ... Jeez, I spend two weeks writing them, then can't get the bloody words out!' He drags on his fag, exhaling from the side of his mouth. 'Where's Peter with that limo – I need a drink ...'

A succession of people I don't know come and congratulate him with kisses, embraces and manly slaps. Some of the straighter ones look perplexed by gay-wedding etiquette, but I guess that's par for the course till they do one on *EastEnders*.

'I'm so relieved,' says Justin. 'I could board the Belfast and shuffle up a gun barrel! Like Cher in that video where she's only wearing sticky tape!'

Which reminds me ...

'Where do you want your pressie?'

'Oh – dunno. Can you bring it to the reception?'

'Sure,' I say, ignoring the droplets of sweat trickling inside my favourite shirt. 'Grab hold of this, Gina. I'll find us a cab …'

CHAPTER EIGHTEEN

The do is at a bar on the other side of the river. The pavements are deserted as our taxi sails through the City. Outside the hours of international commerce, it's practically a ghost town around here. Our venue is in a shrubby oasis surrounded by railings and imposing buildings. It shares the little park with a bowling green, on which a gentle Saturday-afternoon tournament is in progress.

'Here we go,' says Gina, taking back the present.

She's spotted a mountain forming in one corner of the room and adds our gift to the avalanche. I grab champagne flutes from a passing tray; there's a bigger crowd here for the informal part of the day, including faces which ring a bell from when Justin and I worked at Javelin Communications. I can spot advertising types a mile off, and there's plenty of them. The rest will be teaching friends or family of Peter's.

The French windows overlooking the green are open to what little breeze there is. The commitment-ceremony crowd party on, against a backdrop of white garbed types stooping over non-slip mats. In *Doctor Who* terms, this collision of two disparate dimensions should result in instant vaporisation, or at least a swirly visual effect. Instead we coexist side by side, though the startling level of cigarette smoke out on the lawn just about does the special-effects department's job for them.

A string quartet is grinding through a smorgasbord of themes as everyone sinks more champagne. Gina has wandered off, which is why she's a boon at occasions like this: she doesn't need her hand holding. We are veterans of this sort of thing; helping each other out when the occasion arises. Granted, some of my work functions have been a bit tedious, but there's always a chance she'll meet an available bloke. And suffice it to say, I've kept her company through enough theatrical bum-numbers to balance it out.

By the fourth glass of bubbly I'm sozzling without restraint, as you do when friends are paying. A knot of ginger relatives conga by at nipple level, as Gina reappears with a plate of pasta salad and buffalo mozzarella. She's obviously been digging.

'See them over there?'

She's indicating two men at the bar. They look like a couple and sound like Brummies. One is older with puffy jowls; the other, sibilantly self-confident.

'Headmasters – the pair of them.' Her tone suggests both victory and defeat. 'Don't see that every day. And they're both on the Atkins diet, which explains the awful breath …'

Gina should be with MI5.

I've got one eye on the three-tier chocolate cake as I rifle the buffet a second time. The other is caught by the slinky, tropical-print frock at my side. It's worn by a lady of generous proportions – the kind who knows that not every straight man pines for a whippet in Manolos. I recognise her instantly, but I'm surprised to see her here.

'Tara! I thought you were in Costa Rica!'

'Hello, Dan,' she says with a squeeze. 'I am, really. This is a flying visit.'

Tara was a good suit in our days at Javelin. She understood the creative work, stood up to the clients and didn't give a stuff about the politics. I remember when I heard she and her bloke were jacking it in to go and live in the tropics; I was overawed/jealous/convinced she was bonkers, all at once. But then those who can, do, while those who can't, talk about it. Tara was always the former.

'So, how's it going out there? Must be, what, three years?'

'Five!' she says, nibbling quiche. 'Uphill for the first couple, but it's great now. We've set up our own businesses – I'm making jewellery, Charlie designs websites for the local traders.'

I remember her Charlie now. Quiet bloke; bit sexy in a crumpled-muso sort of way. The kind of guy who Gina could—

'We love it out there. We're building our own place on the edge of the rainforest. One more winter and it's finished!'

I'm not absolutely sure what Costa Rica looks like, so my mind defaults to the island in *Jurassic Park*. I see Tara and Charlie on a veranda, threading beads and tinkering with laptops, to a backdrop of cicadas and squawking pterodactyls.

'How about you – what you been up to since Javelin?'

Even a dozen holidays, gratuitous sex and a decent pay-off can't compete with relocation to the rainforest.

'Oh, you know, plodding on … Scotch eggs are good, aren't they?'

Tara nods. She's on her third. 'That's what I do miss. English grub. Matter of fact, I was in Zoltie's with a few of the Javelin girls on Thursday. They still do the herb-crusted turbot …'

Zoltie's bistro is a favourite of agency account handlers wanting to wine and dine a client somewhere swish. It has the posh, London ambience that clients appreciate when they're up for the day from Hemel Hempstead.

'Funnily enough,' she says, licking a finger, 'I was thinking of you while I was there …'

'Me? Was it the turbot?'

'No, it was tastier than that – only joking! One of the girls was talking about that guy you used to see. Lovely blue eyes, worked in I.T. – what was his name?'

'Anthon- … er, Tony.'

'That's him! Got sacked for couriering spliff on the company motorbike. You still in touch with him?'

'No. Not for years. What did she say about him?'

'She still hears about him through a friend-of-a-friend – I think it's their dealer, actually! Apparently Tony's running some weird gothic restaurant in – god, what's it called …'

I'm not sure I want to know. Like that'll stop me.

'Here or abroad?'

'No, abroad. One of those new Balkan countries. Place with a funny name – always makes me think of Andy Pandy's girlfriend …'

We're on my territory now. 'Looby Loo?'

'Ljubljana! Knew I'd get there!' Tara sighs, with a miniature rock-fall of breadcrumbs. 'Uh-oh – talking of other halves, I'd better go and rescue mine!'

Charlie is over by the string quartet. He looks tanned but otherwise much the same as five years ago. He and Gina are chattering away like marmosets. You can't fault her for effort, but Gina has a knack for picking a loser.

I can't bear to watch as Tara steams over, so I go and find the happy couple. Peter is talking to his mum, explaining something with a champagne flute flecked with pith. Justin is slumped on a sofa, top button undone and grinning like a lottery winner. Beside him is Amelie, looking wobbly. She's still in that hat.

I'm coming round to this partnership-registration business. At first I thought it was kowtowing to convention, but now I feel quite proud of my mates for grasping the new respectability. Justin and Peter are homely souls, no big-time banner carriers for the cause. Yet in their quiet way, in front of work colleagues, friends and relatives, they've made a bigger stand than I ever have.

'Cheers, Justin,' I say as he raises his glass for a clink. 'How does it feel to be married?'

'Expensive!' he grimaces. But he doesn't mean it.

Out on the green, old bowlers start to weary. The day wears on through speeches, polite embarrassment and cake. The buffet is devastated and the party thins to a diehard core. As the string quartet takes a fidgety swipe at 'Danny Boy', Peter's rellies get down to their shirtsleeves on the dance floor. Amelie is back on her feet, demonstrating a step involving a 180-degree turn that leaves her headgear undisturbed.

I catch Gina's eye. Time to air-kiss our way out.

CHAPTER NINETEEN

I never did get that Sunday roast.

Anthony isn't Anthony. Anthony is Tony – or he used to be. And he's sure as shit not an account director at Radius Direct. In advertising, you don't go from I.T. monkey to top account banana in under a year, no matter how pretty you are.

Without giving him another look, I turn and walk back across the Common.

Isn't this just my luck? I meet a guy who is hot, keen and available: guaranteed he's a liar and/or fruitcake! Though I've only his word for it he's single.

'*I am single!*'

We're back at my flat, lunch forgotten. He's on the settee looking uncomfortable; I'm standing, to avoid sharing the same upholstery.

'Why should I believe you? You've lied about everything else!'

He gives me some crapola about being 'Tony' at work and 'Anthony' out of it. It's all bollocks. He's not to be trusted.

Oh, and I was right when I thought I'd seen him before. Just the once and only a glimpse – about a year ago. It was in Soho, on my first day at Javelin Communications; lunchtime at the Camel & Star. Sandra had gone off to recce the area for overpriced exercise options, so I was trying to bond with my new workmates over a pint and sausage sandwich at the creatives' favoured pub.

They seemed like an affable lot, the Javelin copywriters and art directors, with a higher proportion of girls than your typically male, hetero & WASPy Creative department. I took to two of the girls immediately. Karen and Sally had been a team since they left uni in Manchester. Both dark-haired and lovely, they had high-flier boyfriends at other agencies, which put them off-limits to their colleagues and earned them the status of Honorary Blokes. By a second beer in their company, my own trace of a Northern accent is falling back into place like the snow on the Pennines.

'They're a nice bunch of lads, but they're not much to look at,' says Sally, who's already spotted which way my bread's buttered. All the male creatives are huddled round a tatty *Baywatch* pinball machine. A couple of them are borderline cute, if not what you'd call snappy dressers. It's all trainers and baggy-knee jeans, with a crumpled tee or sweatshirt.

'They're here every lunchtime,' says Karen, following my eyes.

A sandy-haired lad on the flippers yells, 'You're rocking it, you arsehole!' to a stream of denials. And every now and then they cheer, as the headboard erupts in a Stylophone rendering of the *Baywatch* theme, and the orange bulbs in Pamela Anderson's bikini light up exactly where you'd expect.

'And then there's Tony, of course – but he's not long for this world,' says Sally, nodding over my shoulder to a padded booth at the end.

And that's when I clock him. Sitting with two or three others at a beer-stained table. I can only see him side-on, but he is quite the handsomest man in the pub: sharp suit, dark-blue eyes, lips that are wasted on supping beer. Everyone around him looks as sombre as he does.

'What's going on there?' I ask, manoeuvring for a better angle.

'He's out on his ear,' says Karen. 'We don't know what for, but he got hauled up by the M.D. this morning. Told to clear his desk and get out.'

'It'll be porn,' says Sally, nodding knowingly. 'You know what I.T. are like. Except it won't be shavenschoolgirls.com. Not in Tony's case …'

She winks at me with a little shrug. 'He's fit, though, eh?'

A minute later, Sandra turns up with the leaflets for four different gyms. Next time I look round, that padded booth is empty.

As I eased into the new job, I remember thinking how I.T. Tony would have made a welcome distraction about the place. But he was never to darken the door of Javelin Communications again. So, intentionally or otherwise, that handsome face slipped to the back of my mind; into a section marked 'Missed Opportunities of the Late Twentieth Century'.

Where it would have stayed, if he hadn't walked onto that dancefloor at Wallops one famous, fateful Saturday night.

CHAPTER TWENTY

It's past six when Gina drops me off. Drinking in the daytime does me in, and I've had more than my quota. I feel lethargic and out of kilter; tipsy when I should be sober, bloated when I'm usually wondering what to have for dinner.

Preoccupied, too, with the spectre of Anthony emerging from the shadows yet again. I'd forgotten our Javelin connection after all these years. It had caused a minor stir when I started seeing him, a year after I joined the agency. But by then, the gravity of his dope-couriering crime had been downgraded to an industry prank. It was the subject of chortled anecdotes, and even got a mention in the M.D.'s speech at the Christmas party.

Then – nothing, till I saw him in Helsinki. If I did see him in Helsinki ... How can he have been there if he was in Ljubljana? Unless he's on some mighty transcontinental tour, spreading his demonic charms among the innocents of Europe. Anyway, wherever he is, if he's there he can't be here. And that's the way I like it.

I slip out of my wedding clothes into baggy shorts, and open up the sitting-room curtains. In the course of the day, the sun tracks round my flat like a slow-motion searchlight, so I shut them to keep the heat out.

I can't decide what to do with myself – stay in, go out, watch a movie, read something – so I switch on the computer while I think about it. Since I last logged off, and gave myself a generous fourteen minutes to shower, shave and dress for my mate's wedding, I've had six new messages.

CRAZEEGUY 10:45, July 26
Hello Mr Hornet my name es Joao
[1] [2] [3] [4]

CHESTERFIELD 11:01, July 26
Hi there nice profile. Do you like Show Tunes?

SPEEDBOY1983 12:22, July 26
Mmmm tasty bloke … what you doing this aft?
Am lkg for fun with 1 or more hot guys.
Brixton can travel or accom.
[1] [2]

MAESTROMAN 15:07, July 26
Hi Dan. See you're not online but catch you soon. Hope you're still having fun in the sun. Glorious isn't it. MM XX

SEXYSAM 15:34, July 26
Hi mate. Great shorts in pic 3. Where you get them?

CHESTERFIELD 18:25, July 26
Hope I didn't scare you off. I also like greyhounds.

I still get a sad little thrill from a stack of messages in my inbox. Like a rustling stocking at the end of the bed on Christmas morning. Of today's trove, two pique my curiosity. MAESTROMAN has been quiet for a while. I left him a couple of messages last week. He hasn't been online, but that's not unusual; he's a lighter click4dicker than I am. And he's never followed through when I've suggested a date, though not in a game-playing way. Some online cruisers are only there for the ego massage, in pursuit of no more than the pleasure of being pursued.

I tap back a message to MAESTROMAN. Say I'm sorry I missed him, and that he'll never guess where I've been this afternoon.

SPEEDBOY1983 is also no longer online. Which is a pity, because it's flattering to be sounded out for meaningless sex by one so young and springy. By the looks of it, I'm old enough to be his father, which may be my appeal. It takes someone like him to remind me I'm nearly forty – and looking at his pics, I can't complain. I imagine a straight man my age has to be considerably richer and/or hotter than I am before the female equivalent of SPEEDBOY1983 invites herself round for a gangbang.

I check the TV guide for distractions. The evening schedule is a mix of fly-on-the-walls, best-ever countdowns and how to sue your plastic surgeon. So I sit awhile and sift profiles instead.

Without the telly on, by eight o'clock I'm conscious of the persistent *thud-thud* from the pub across the junction. It's a popular pick-up joint, and from where I'm sitting I've got a clear view of the beer terrace. On summer evenings it's heaving way beyond factory-farming guidelines, with a typical, straight South London crowd: boys and girls, black and white, gaggling in clusters. The pub is a thorn in the flesh of us local residents; more so with all the current talk of extending licensing hours, and it's not just because of the noise. That impromptu walled terrace sprung up overnight the summer before last, without so much as planning permission. The local council insist they're looking into it – and right now, I feel duty-bound to join them …

For on hot, still nights like this, the shirts are off; and with their tattoos and their gymmed-up torsos, the straight lads are united in shaven-headed splendour. The bouncers, in their summer uniform of tight black T-shirts and shades, are keeping a watchful eye. They have necks like stacks of tyres, and enough electronics in one ear to supervise an emergency landing on the Common.

Forget what I said about not feeling my age. You know you're getting on when you come out with things your gran used to say … Thirty years ago, when my brother grew his hair to match his Captain Beefheart poster, she said, '*You can't tell the boys from the girls these days* …' Gawping at this soft-core panorama across the road, I know how she felt; half the time, I can't tell gay and straight men apart any more. I blame David Beckham, and a stealthy coterie of designers for whipping men's fashion into a whirl of sexual confusion. Marrying stubbly scalps to impossible prettiness and gravity-defying waistbands to lank sumo locks, the straight boys on the terrace look just like the guys down the Barrel & Tap. Though, I have to say, they're better at vaulting a three-foot wall than I am … I wonder if they see the irony; and how their girlfriends see through it, savvy to a code that beats me …

Oops, one of the bouncers catches me ogling!

Just as my favourite chocolate-brown Labrador saunters into view, taking her owner to the Common.

My eyes follow her round the corner, pretending it was the dog I was watching all along.

Bad boy, I sigh; straight men are strictly for the birds ...

I pull back from the glass, grateful not for the first time that my window cleaner does inside as well as out.

*

The last empty Fosters can misses the bin at twenty past midnight. In six hours I have sent 105 messages and conversed with twenty-two men. I've been invited to have sex five times, to attend a threesome in Chiswick (counts as two), and to discuss my preferred use of candlewax with a vet in Harrow. So far, I've resisted them all.

At about this time, online numbers tend to dwindle as randy punters give up and head for their nearest club. I could do the same, of course; join Duncan at the Barrel from where he texted me an hour ago. I should, too; get out and swarm with the barflies, instead of sitting here stalking alone. Thing is, I can't be arsed; the tubes have shut, so anywhere beyond short-range means a call, a cab and hassle, hassle (*tight git*), hassle.

Of course, there's always the possibility of a home delivery. But that goes against my personal safety rules, especially at night. And anyway, I'm not horny enough to do anything that dodgy. Yet.

My most tempting offer was from BIG_SEAN in Streatham. Net cruisers come up with the oddest monikers, but there's no arguing with a six-and-a-half-foot skinhead called BIG_SEAN – about his name or anything else. He's quite sexy in a scary BNP-activist sort of way, but that's an image he's quick to dispel. Under 'Looking For' he's written 'Black guyz, white guyz, know-how-to-fuck guyz'; and his private pictures show him in flagrante with an unidentified man who looks like Frank Bruno minus the Lurex shorts.

BIG_SEAN was a long shot when I messaged him, but for a while he seemed quite keen. I look a bit moody myself in some of my pictures (notably one where I'd just put my wallet through the boil wash), so we batted messages back and forth for a while. Turned out he was up for a drink and taking it from there. But then I got:

> BIG_SEAN 10:48, July 26
> By the way mate do you bareback

I recheck his profile, and sure enough he's left the 'Safe Sex' box blank. It's usually the first thing I check, but by now I'm slacking. Condom use is a sticky issue these days, with HIV positive guys rebelling by ditching the condoms in favour of personal freedom and a hotter, badder fuck. Since I've always preferred the jiggery to the actual pokery, it's not that much of an issue for me. But from what click4dick-ers put in their profiles, I know it's rife.

By the sound of it I'm way too vanilla for BIG_SEAN. So I make my excuses and say I'm off to bed.

He responds with:

> BIG_SEAN 11:02, July 26
> Yeah yeah I'll be down the Skip in Vauxhall if
> you change your mind. Piss night, my
> favourite.

(Tempting, but …)

I wonder what The Boys are doing tonight. Half of me wants to see if they're online, but I can't bring myself to disbar their profile. When we got back from Helsinki, I made it invisible to my machine. It was the right thing to do. Just a pity you can't do it with people.

With the beer all gone and a good-natured fuzz in my head, I'm thinking about going to bed for real. But by now I'm horribly, *horribly* horny; which means I have to either a) find a cheap, sleazy prick-teaser like the ones I'm always running down, for a bit of instant-message net-sturbation; or b) dim the lights and load up a DVD.

Recourse to porn is the lazy option. It lacks the intimate, human dimension of jerking off at the keyboard with an ephemeral nobody, though as a rule, the dicks are bigger. I can watch porn the way straight men watch football (I can also watch football the way straight men watch porn) and tonight is one of those nights. So there I am, about to pick out my celluloid cocksman of choice from the stack above the CDs; when, in one of those weird flashes of serendipity that happens but once or twice a lifetime, a celluloid cocksman picks me.

> *AARON.SHADWICK 00:24, July 27*
> *In Chelsea if you fancy a fuck.*

Like any gay man with a porn collection big enough to interest Sotheby's, I immediately suspect a wind-up. Aaron Shadwick is a legend; one of the few Brits ever to make it in L.A. He started making movies Stateside about ten years ago, giving them his best shot and taking quite a few in return. In the process, he became the Jeff Stryker of the nineties: part of a new generation of porno beefcake, following the rise of safe sex and the demise of the pudding-bowl haircut. He's made a career out of man-on-man hardcore – sometimes *men*-on-man hardcore – and I can't see him chatting me up on a Saturday night.

My fingers are quivering as I click to his details. Three photos, at least one of which I've seen on a video cover. Well, that proves nothing – I could have scanned those in myself. Under 'Occupation' he's put 'Actor/ Model/Artist'. And under 'Safe Sex': 'Always'.

Height, weight, colour of hair and eyes ... Yep, everything you'd put if you wanted to pass yourself off as Aaron Shadwick. And what about:

'Dick Size: Extra Large'.

Get away!

Celebs are not unknown on click4dick. I've chatted to the odd second-rate pop star myself, and Duncan had a drink with an ex-*Blue Peter* presenter.

But this ... ?

I feel my heart in my chest as I type.

> *HORNYDSW4 00:27, July 27*
> *are u **the** aaron shadwick? as in jailbreak jerk-off, and rodeo party I, II & III?*

> *AARON.SHADWICK00:29, July 27*
> *Thats the one. Fancy a fuck or not.*

Gosh. I wonder if the F-word is generic, or if by taking up his offer I'll be expected to take up considerably more where the sun don't shine. Ask any gay man with a porn habit how he fancies being on the receiving end of Aaron Shadwick, and he'll break into a hot flush or cold sweat, subject to preference.

Outside, a police siren blares by, switching down the whoop-selector from *Starsky & Hutch* to *Strangled Turkey* in a show of neighbourly consideration. It is half-past midnight. I am sozzled. I am horny. I am contemplating a liaison with someone on the net who claims to be a living legend of porn. Someone who may, in fact, be a queer-basher. Or queer-bashers plural. Or terribly fat.

There is protocol, even among slappers. Under normal circumstances, I'd insist on meeting in a bar; or on a well-lit street corner, if he looks really hot and in a hurry. Either would verify his identity before I disappeared behind closed doors.

But this – is – Aaron – Shadwick!

Maybe.

It's either madness or a dream come true. I need to keep a level head, think carefully and weigh up the situation in a responsible manner.

There is a feeling I've come to recognise in myself in situations like this. One that makes the rational course of action irrelevant, because I know for a fact I'm going to do the opposite.

AARON.SHADWICK 00:33, July 27
Last chance mate. Do you want the address.

I particularly get it when I'm drunk.

CHAPTER TWENTY-ONE

Tremorne House in Rochester Walk isn't what I imagined. Even in the gloom the location is amazing: one street back from the Thames, and another from whitewashed semis with gables and gardens and topiarised privacy. The houses are smart but not spectacular. Anywhere else, they'd imply a comfy Middle-England lifestyle; here they stand for nothing less than old money and showbiz stardom.

Yet no matter how chi-chi the curtains or well-kept the borders, every west-facing window is cursed with a view of Tremorne House. Like just about everywhere in London, Chelsea has its share of carbuncles, and this one is pure council. It is a concrete block cast from concrete blocks, with railings and walkways, and a stairwell that needs the whiff of piss to set it off like the Queen needs a handbag.

I pay the cabbie. A cat scoots by and leaps silently into the hedge on the moneyed side of the street. The breeze plays off the river as I climb the kind of dank, unlit stairs that cops charge up in gritty TV dramas. The lack of litter or spray paint suggests someone is trying to keep up with the Hon. Joneses; but the bars on every window are inescapably municipal, despite the potted flowers peeking valiantly through the grilles like Death Row inmates in their Sunday best.

Ten – eleven … and this is it. As I rap on the knocker a security light pops on. A wire disappears through a crack above the door; it seems Mr Shadwick has a way with electrical appliances. Which, now I think about it, is no surprise.

There is a long pause. I feel for the comfort of the keys in my pocket. I'm wondering which way to go to find another thirteen-quid taxi, when the door opens onto a dim hallway. A face and one hefty, naked pectoral appear round the edge of the door frame.

'Dan, right?'

The voice is raspingly authentic, if minus the trademark mid-Atlantic drawl. But no two ways about it: this is Aaron Shadwick.

He looks older than I expect. But then the image I carry in my head is from films he made ten years ago. His profile says he is thirty-three, but I'd say he is nearer my age. I suddenly realise I don't know if he still makes films, or if he gave them up to become a walking, talking portrait in the attic of gay consciousness.

He's wearing bobbly grey tracksuit bottoms and – clearly – nothing else. I follow him across the uncarpeted hall to the lounge. In one corner is an open sofa bed, hastily dressed in a duvet of porn-set garishness. I feel like I've seen it before, and check the corners for wall-mounted cameras. But then maybe bedlinen is a perk of his job; part of the spoils to be divvied up at the end of the shoot, with the left-over lube and the Daddy, Mummy and Baby Bear-sized butt plugs.

''Scuse the mess,' he says as I hover in the doorway. 'I'm borrowing this place. D'you want a beer?'

He reappears with two cans from behind a beaded curtain, which settles back into a Warhol-style potato print of Princess Di. It's the first time I get a decent look at him. His hair is grizzled salt and pepper, straggling over his ears. But he still has the torso of a drill sergeant, and the jaw of a rowing blue. Two out of three reasons why the camera loved him.

Handing me a beer and cracking open his own, he sits at the laptop in the corner which is providing much of the light. I can see over his shoulder he's still on click4dick. A steady stream of electronic beeps indicate incoming messages. I'm disappointed he hasn't logged off, and the fact he's still messaging makes me uneasy. What exactly is my status in the night's proceedings: entrée or hors d'oeuvre?

He walks back over and stands an inch from my nose.

'You've still got your clothes on,' he says, in what I suspect counts for foreplay. I still can't believe this is happening.

You get a bit blasé about bumping into celebs where I live. A *Big Brother* winner walks past my flat all the time, and I'm in the same Sainsbury's Local catchment area as two alternative comedians. But actual one-to-one encounters are rare, beyond the sets and voice-over studios that go with my job. And even there, I've never once seen Hannah Gordon stripped to the waist, sporting a nipple ring.

I sense preliminaries are dispensed with, so I go to kiss the unsmiling lips. They are warm but unresponsive. I try a gentle tweak of his nipples and get a better reception. They are classically, enviably beautiful, the way men's nipples are meant to be. He has both my T-shirts off in a second, and begins to return the interest.

Keen as I am to notch up a night of passion with Aaron Shadwick, I am genuinely curious to meet the real person. But conversation plays little part in his porn persona, and he's staying determinedly in character. I sense all he wants is to flex the muscles of his own fiction – and that tonight, the lucky punter invited on set, is me.

I smell his breath. Feel his stubble against my cheek. By the impeccable standards of the porn fraternity, his body is a little gone-to-seed. But it retains the rubbery hardness of the naturally athletic. If he ever did steroids, he did them well.

He tugs my drawstring, I tug his drawstring … And before I know it, I am butt naked on a mangy sofa bed in Chelsea, with my hand round one of the most famous dicks in the world. A dick you can buy in sex shops, cast in pink latex. I know, because Duncan was given one as a leaving gift, with a scrotum that feels exactly like the wrist-rest I use for my RSI.

The original is bristlier. In fact, the whole of Aaron Shadwick is earthily unwaxed, and all the better for it. In his early movies he was primped and glossed to a doll-like prettiness, with as much Vaseline on his pouty lips as other, more frictional areas. But for all it lacks in smoothness his skin is still exquisite – blemished by nothing but the dexterity that inked a seahorse into the small of his back. It peers from between delicate twin dints at the base of his spine that were made to hold cocaine at a depraved bacchanalia, and surely have.

We intertwine, but he seems detached. I suspect he's had more than beer, though I couldn't hazard a guess at what. Hard drugs frighten me, and in avoiding them I've also avoided learning much about them. I know plenty of people dabble without ill effect. But now I'm feeling uneasy again; snared in the increasingly sweaty grip of a man who is mumbling aggressively, whose attention is drifting from the matter in hand. I know my nerves are showing when my left eye tosses in a few extra blinks. They're showing somewhere else, too.

'D'you want half a Viagra?' he asks.

Uh-oh. It's make-your-mind-up time: *Lose face and chance of a lifetime to shag Aaron Shadwick* versus *Accept drugs from total stranger who is very probably out of his tree already.*

Tricky one ... No surprise he has Viagra; it's everywhere, including my email inbox at least twice a day. Porn stars are said to pop it for enhanced performance, like marathon runners minus the random testing.

He breaks the little blue diamond in two and gives me half. Holds his beer to my lips until it's gone. Then takes the other half himself, though he hardly needs it.

It is not unknown for my ardour to desert me when I'm less than completely at ease. But half a Viagra makes all the difference. In minutes, my inhibitions are dispelled, replaced with a new sense of purpose once the effects are firmly visible.

I am here – right now – and I am going to do this!

And, yeah, it does feel sleazy and it does feel cold. But it also feels hot and sexy and very, very exciting. There is not a gay man alive who would knock back Aaron Shadwick – and I am very alive indeed.

He doesn't do much. Lies there while I have my way. I wonder what's going on in his head as I grind against him – this guy who gets paid to fuck with angels, who is doing it with me.

Why is he?

And, bollocks, no, I don't have a self-esteem problem. I know I'm no warthog, but I'm no Adonis either. But the truth is, if I was him I'd think I was slumming it.

When I'm done, I lie there beside him. If this was one of his movies, it's when we would kiss one last, intense time, camera zooming in on our flushed and satiated faces. But in real life he's not big on kissing – before or after. And anyway, we have unfinished business.

'You're all right,' he says, pushing my hand away. 'I don't want to come yet.'

His dick is still primed, tin-can hard and uncannily familiar. I've done my duty and I think I'm about to be dismissed.

Aaron Shadwick sits up and swigs the last of his beer. He lobs the empty through the curtain, at a bag on the kitchen floor. I watch the mystic totem of his cock as it bobs out of reach, on its way back to the laptop.

That's that, then.

I unpeel myself from the duvet. 'The bathroom is, er … ?'

'First left. Do us a favour – bin the condom.'

Talk about clearing up after yourself.

When I come back, he's sifting through a torrent of messages. Stops at one and taps his address into a blank message box beneath a picture I recognise. Big blond French guy, hung like Hanratty. Lives in Crouch End with his motorbike. I've tried to spark his interest a dozen times and never got more than a monosyllable.

I'm leaning on Mr Shadwick's chunky shoulder, wondering if now is the time to mention my proficiency at threesomes. With the tiniest shrug, he says:

'Sorry, mate. You better get dressed.'

I take my phone out of my trainer where I stowed it. Time is 03:18.

I didn't expect croissants and *The Archers* omnibus, but it would have been cool to stay the night. Isn't bedding a porn star one of those things you're meant to do before you're forty? Like driving a Ferrari and visiting the Galápagos? Maybe this experience isn't going to have quite the kudos I anticipated, but it's something to tell the grandchildren. Theoretically.

'Where's the best place to get a cab?' I ask.

'Down by the river,' he says, half turning to look at me with what might be sheepishness. 'You got enough cash?'

It is a very good point. I empty the change out of my pocket. Nine quid.

I can't deny it feels like a little victory: taking money from a sex-industry legend when you've just climbed out of his bed. He pulls on his trackie bottoms, turns over the duvet – which I think could have waited till I'd gone. Then he shows me to the door.

He's more relaxed now, almost friendly, head nodding to an inaudible beat.

'Cheers, then,' he says as he turns the double lock.

'Cheers, Aaron,' I say. And I kiss his sandpaper cheek.

'Cheers …' He looks less sure.

I hang around at the first set of lights and hail a cab in minutes. The traffic is thin as we whisk back across Chelsea Bridge. Out of the side window the moon is a sliver; at its furthest wane from that fullness in which I, alone, can see the triumphant face of Margaret Thatcher, frozen in sink-the-Belgrano oratory. The lights from houseboats and tower blocks streak the river like phosphorescence. I text Duncan, tell him I'm safely on my way home. He can't have picked up my last one yet; it is inconceivable he'd have nothing to say.

Even now, my heart is beating more than it should.

I did it. I shagged Aaron Shadwick!

Most of the time I felt he was humouring me. Like the captain of the football team, letting the kit man have a kick-about.

Fuck it, though, eh? It was his idea!

It's a shame black cabs have security screens these days. For once, I quite fancy a chat: *Here, mate! You'll never guess who the bloke in the back of your cab just had!*

The very first time I met an actor who had played *Doctor Who*, I rushed home to listen to my treasured audio tape of his best-ever story. I'll be following the same principle tonight as I slip in my DVD of *Street Stud II: Director's Cut*.

Part homage, part curiosity and partly this sodding Viagra.

CHAPTER TWENTY-TWO

It is the beginning of August and I've nearly forgotten I used to work at all. The redundancy money is lasting better than expected. The bit I get from the dole stops it going down too fast, and it's amazing how little you can live on when the alternative feels as grim as returning to office life.

As a weary nine-to-fiver, an expanse of time all to yourself is a veritable nirvana. Something you can only dream of when you're lashed to the treadmill of the working week. But by now the weeks are blurring, one into the next, and even the days lose their identity. My life is my own on a Wednesday as much as a Saturday. If anything, the weekends are a bit of a let-down; it's the only time I feel squeezed back into the mould of real life, as the streets and shops and bars are swamped with other escapees.

The weather, like Lionel Shanks, has been unwittingly kind. It is turning out to be a summer like the ones in children's fiction. Opening my curtains on a bright-blue sky never ceases to delight, and sometimes I just fall right back on the bed like Doris Day. Where, if I keep still, I can fix my eyes on the flight path and watch a different plane plough into my window frame every ninety seconds.

When I was working, annual leave was priceless, and making the most of it an obligation. To me, twenty-five days a year meant twenty-five days abroad, packing in the scene-changes like staying home was heresy. Sure, I could have blown my entire pay-off on a big beast of a holiday, when in fact I haven't been away since Helsinki. Dunc and I keep talking about last-minute deals, though I can't keep his mind off flats for long enough to do anything about it. Yet even lying here, watching the jets come in, I have to say I've no regrets about staying put and spinning out the money.

For on days like this, the world is mine – and I can do anything. I've never been one for lazing in bed, so I'm up by half-eight most days. And if I'm going somewhere, I make a pact with myself to be out by 10 a.m., to keep me off click4dick. A day can vanish all too easily when you're hunkered down like a polar bear at a breathing hole, waiting for something sleek and tasty to pop its head out. Today I manage it: out of the house by 9.45. It's Tuesday and I'm going to the gym. Nothing special about that, but I'm thinking later I'll have a bit of culture. A museum maybe, or an exhibition. There's a Jean Paul Gaultier retrospective at the V & A – or is it Yves Saint Laurent? Either way, it's more me than Tate Modern, and I bet they're doing lovely souvenir T-shirts.

My deal at New York Fitness runs out in three weeks, so I'm yomping into town via the Common. The sun is shining, the grass is greenish, and fifty-five minutes in a backpack at a healthy lick means I can forgo the cardio when I get there – win-win-win. At the children's playground, yummy mummies spill out of the clapboard clubhouse in full make-up and designer combat gear. A remarkable proportion are pregnant, which goes for the ladies of Clapham in general; some days, I can sit in Starbucks and count more expecting than not. It's as if the summer air makes them swell up like muffins.

All is well with the world on the Common. Squirrels are foraging between the trees, capering with roller-coaster grace. As I pass the bandstand a skein of geese flies overhead. The graffiti and rotting roof planks give it the air of a dilapidated pier, and I wonder when it last played host to anything more than skateboarders.

I'm in sight of the road when my phone rings. Which is a nuisance, because it's hard to hear with the traffic, and if I slow down from a yomp I won't get the cardio benefit. A name flashes up on the display. Oh God – Shelley Pembridge!

'Hi, Shelley …'

'Dan, darling, how are you?'

'I'm really well – just strolling in the sunshine …' (Having a lovely time, thanks, Shell.)

'Lucky you, lucky you … Listen, darling, I won't keep you dangling. Just wanted to touch base vis-à-vis availability for work … Grady Buscott are crying out for writers – and I'm having lunch with your old mate Gavin Horner, who's just joined Warp Direct as E.C.D., with a remit to take on three senior teams …'

Shelley Pembridge is the hairiest woman in advertising. She is one of those headhunters who doesn't talk to you for years, then phones up like you were sharing a back wax only yesterday. She is famous for having her finger off the pulse; and, while she did admittedly strike gold by getting me my first job in the business, she has struck only clinker since. Today, she is wide of the mark on two counts, having mistaken me for someone who a) gives a flying one about vacancies at a sweatshop like Grady Buscott, and b) classes Gavin Horner as an 'old mate'.

''Fraid I'm not on the market just yet, Shelley.

Probably give it another month or so, before I look around ... But thanks for thinking of me!'

She maintains her arch diplomacy, though this is clearly not what she wants to hear.

'*Well, as you like, my love – but I wouldn't leave it too long.*' There is a shuffle of papers, presumably my CV. '*You're coming up to forty now, aren't you? At that difficult stage ... Time to decide if you're built for the big jobs ...*'

I tell her I am sure she's right and that I'll give it some thought. Then I plead poor reception and say goodbye; this is not a day for talking big jobs with Shelley Pembridge.

At the edge of the Common I pass between the two grand terraces that allegedly caused Queen Victoria such grief – if you believe she had the capacity for more. I take the route to the gym that involves the fewest road-crossings, and today the pelicans are in my favour.

Advertising headhunters thrive by having the inside track on people and agencies. So how Shelley makes any money, if she thinks I'm the sort of name to drop into the polenta with Gavin Horner, I cannot imagine. The fact he's landed the executive creative director's job at Warp Direct is galling, but no surprise. In my business, people like him shaft their way to the top all the time.

The quickest route to New York Fitness takes me past the front door of Chartwell Shanks, but I've taken to going another way. The sight of the agency's whey-faced smokers, grabbing a minute's poisoned respite on the steps, is one illicit pleasure I'm reluctant to allow myself too often. Once I'm in the gym, I spend my workout trying not to think about Horner ... He's an ex-boss of ours and definitely not a mate, though I nearly considered him one once. His management style was black and white: he loved you or he hated you, and luckily I was in the first category, at least for a year or two. Then something changed. Suddenly my work was shit, and Sandra and I were getting all the dud briefs. I was invisible when he passed me in the corridor, conspicuously excluded from his little jokes.

Gavin Horner was a man's man, and not in the way I like. He was into motorbikes and hiking up volcanoes. He was also happily married with kids. But his change of heart was so unheralded, yet so complete, I began to wonder if he had a thing for me and couldn't handle it. Preposterous, probably – immodest, definitely – but it made as much sense as anything. My work wasn't shit, no matter what he said, or if it was, it was the same shit it had always been. I was convinced he was gunning for me, to the point where I kept records of all his slights, ready to argue for constructive dismissal if it came to it. In the end, Sandra and I got a better job first. It's a chapter of my life I was glad to close, though not before I challenged him … When I went into his office to hand in my notice, I asked him why he'd been like this. Horner spluttered, feigning incomprehension, all wide eyes and wider hands, like a footballer protesting innocence to the ref: *How could I say such a thing?* How, when we'd always got on so well, had *he* gone from hero to zero in *my* eyes?

He managed to turn it all around – accused me of the injustice that he was guilty of, to the point where I started to question myself. It was a talent that frightened me, and I hated him for it. Not least because I'd encountered it once before.

CHAPTER TWENTY-THREE

Anthony and I lasted five months, from beginning to dead end. I never imagined your feelings for someone could switch from one extreme to the other so quickly.

The speed with which he wore himself a niche in my life was extraordinary, but at the time I was a soft option for any persistent tide. Despite his promises, the half-truths and inconsistencies continued, all of which I glossed over in an attractive shade of lust. Putting it simply, Anthony was the most attractive human being I had ever met. Like a seventies ad for aftershave, I had the feral urge to rip every stitch of clothing from his body the second he walked through the door. It was a passion he claimed to share, though before long the evidence was scant.

Not that it mattered. I had enthusiasm enough for two, and that carried us along for a while. Besides, he scored so well in other categories I could ignore his reticence. He was perfect long-term boyfriend material. He had the knack of hitting it off with strangers, and not just ones who wanted to jump all over him. When I introduced him to my friends (colleagues were hardly an option) within five minutes they'd be chatting away, his body language boasting of old acquaintance. And domestically he was a god, at least at first. His duck à l'orange was exquisite – a revelation to my oven, the sophistication of which was wasted on a heat-it-up-scrape-it-off man like me. Bar the times I'd used it to dry my trainers, Anthony was the first to put its grill/fan/convection capabilities to the test.

He could erect an IKEA flat-pack in the time it took me to count up for stray components. He tackled those last, nagging jobs around the flat that had eluded my attention – like stripping the layers of paint from the glass panels of my kitchen door. He would sit cross-legged on a Sunday afternoon, fitting draft excluders to the bottom of doors; I would bring tea and sit beside him as he kneeled, too absorbed in his job to notice how the shirt, untucking itself from the back of his jeans, was making me fantastically aroused. Take it from me: it's not easy to feign interest in DIY when all you're thinking about is Doing Him Yourself.

In these and other respects, Anthony was an ideal husband. In public, his displays of affection were impeccable. He was never slow to slip an affectionate hand into my back pocket, initially even when it was empty. And, while I evidently didn't light his candle with the same flame-thrower zeal, I never caught his eye or other part of his delectable anatomy wandering anywhere it shouldn't.

'Which way are we going?' he'd say as the bedside lamp clicked off.

Should he snuggle into my back, or me into his? Usually the former, since pressing myself against his torso and those mango-firm buttocks inevitably meant sleep eluded me. So I would turn away as he cleaved to me with smooth restraint. I remember once, waking with a start at 3 a.m. to the wail of a car alarm outside. His body was exactly where he'd left it; still cradling me, like the ejector seat of a pilot coming-to on a dark hillside.

This relative idyll lasted a matter of weeks, its life cycle accelerated by Anthony's irresistible keenness to move into my flat. This went against my better judgement – and the advice of friends. Receptive and flattered as I was, I couldn't help wondering why he wanted to see so much of me, so soon. It was my own fault for handing over what Duncan calls the 'B.C. key' (Boyfriend's Copy) in record time. Before I knew it, Anthony and I had lapsed from passionate dating to numb domesticity. We never officially called it 'living together', though the nights he spent at his mother's place became fewer and farther between.

Prior to this, I had left him to let himself out one Friday morning. I was heading up north after work, to spend the weekend with my parents. Once or twice I called the house in Beckenham and got his mum. A laconic, reedy-voiced woman whom I never met, she said she hadn't seen him. News that sparked my paranoia, till I got back home on the Sunday night, to be greeted by an aroma of roast beef and Yorkshire pud, and a slowly unravelled confession that he'd never left my flat at all.

I was suspicious, but also in love – with the idea of settling down, if not with the man himself. I told him we had to put the brakes on.

'It's too much, too soon,' I said. 'We'll burn ourselves out if we see each other all the time. Lose the—'

(Did I really say *magic*?)

Anthony just smiled. He fixed me with his china-blue eyes and told me not to worry. Then he stuck his hand up my T-shirt and launched himself on top of me, in a calculated seduction he knew I couldn't resist.

That was the start. Sex became a bargaining chip. The spontaneity vanished as he took control, and it coincided with another disappearance: his job at Radius

Direct, assuming it ever existed. What had sounded so impressive the night we met turned out to be maternity cover; a temporary position, followed by another at a different agency, and another. He became cagey about where he was working and what he was doing; preferred to call me at my office rather than give me his work number.

Our evenings began to follow a pattern. When I got home, he'd be there already, cooking supper with food I'd paid for. We would eat and I would wash up. Then I'd find him in the sitting room in his favoured position: slumped on the floor, back against the settee, rolling a spliff in front of the telly. Spliff and telly, telly and spliff; it was all he did. He didn't seem to have hobbies, or many friends of his own. He said he'd been in a band once, could play guitar, but I never saw any proof.

At first, I'd share a joint to keep him company – reluctantly. I couldn't get over the acrid taste, and the jagged high left me befuddled, which I soon learned was unwise. So he'd smoke it himself and then roll another, all the while staring at the TV, laughing at nothing much. And I would lie on the settee, watching the back of his head till it was time to go to bed.

He got into the habit of staying up later and later, getting stoned-er and stoned-er. Sometimes he had nothing to get up for as the temp jobs became sporadic. But I was convinced it was also a ploy to avoid what he considered my insatiable desire – because, even oafish and unresponsive, he still did it for me.

He abandoned the pretence of sharing my exercise regime after two sessions of playing the buffed-up, corn-fed couple at the gym. Yet not even his early-onset paunch softened my enthusiasm – if anything, it inflamed it. Particularly when teamed with his ancient blue-hooped rugby jersey, with the indelible mud stains and the hole in one elbow. This was his favourite slobbing-around gear, a remnant of his schooldays in the First XV (he said). It was a matter of pride he could still fit into it, and his nascent belly seemed only to add to the authenticity. As far as I was concerned, Anthony was the kind of guy who looked hot in anything. I couldn't take Dunc and Gina seriously when they said they didn't see it; how unlike my best buddies to lie! It pains me to say it, but I put it down to jealousy – poor things.

Anthony, well aware of the sexual thrall he held me, played on it ruthlessly. The more he rationed the bedroom business, the more I fell for it. Sexually, I was still finding my way in those pre-net days, and he could set me begging with a single look. Give or take a love handle, Anthony was blessed with a fine physique, which failed to desert him no matter how much he neglected it. If ever he riled me, all it took was a few lazy press-ups to transform his torso into a glossy, vein-marbled object of veneration. And my anger, if not forgotten, was at least averted.

Besotted as I was, I knew we weren't built to last. It would take a greater self-deluder than I to trust Anthony Duke beyond a point. The honeymoon period was lightning fast; he tossed the L-word my way as hastily as I passed the door key his. The significance of both gestures eroded as quickly, the implicit trust devalued. He had a profound talent for reading my moods; he could defuse me on a bad day – after a hellish journey home on the tube, say – make me see my fury for the absurdity it was. But as his jobs became intermittent, I learned not to harp on about my own. His past at Javelin was a no-go area, which was a shame because I had lots of questions. And on the odd occasion something so momentous or hilarious happened at work that I couldn't resist repeating it, he would gasp or laugh at the punchline as required, faking nonchalance. But the backlash was never far behind, erupting from the guise of another matter an hour later, or a day.

In a skewing of reality that established another pattern, it became apparent the one with the shameful association with Javelin was me. Whether it was my relative success at the scene of his ignominious firing, or the fact I was holding down a job at all, my life began to displease Anthony. I found myself in the improbable position of being his lover, provider, magnanimous landlord (no rent was offered) and enemy within. I started to feel tolerated; kept at arm's-length by the man sharing my bed. He could swing from angel to demon in a moment; it was as if he'd found a secret panel in my flat through which he and his malevolent twin swapped places at will.

Anthony wasn't the brightest guy I'd ever met, but he had a way with words that left me standing. He was a twister of the truth, a manipulator of the argument who could shift the grounds of my reasoning till I felt guilty for making a perfectly fair point. Bludgeon me into seeing things his way when, two minutes before, my own perspective had been clear. I'd end up apologising for things I'd never said. I was trapped in a Hitchcock plot, being slowly convinced that I was the mad one. In the end, I'd feel sick – exhausted by sparring with someone who was systematically feeding my brains into a shredder.

Then the money started disappearing from my wallet. The first time, I dismissed it; blamed my memory, or a mix-up at the till. But soon the only explanation was the obvious one – and I had no option but to confront him.

*

The kitchen door was off its hinges, lying on the tiles for the easier scraping of white, then brown, then white paint off its frosted panels. Days ago, Anthony had launched into the task with brio; now, typically, his enthusiasm was on the wane. As the week rolled by, the acrid smell of paint stripper has been replaced by the whiff of spliff as I come through the door each night, foretelling his lack of progress.

He is slumped at the kitchen table, thumbing through the *Evening Standard*.

'Anthony … Did you borrow some money?'

His chin dips to his chest but his eyes stay on the entertainment section.

'How d'you mean?'

'Well, I'm twenty quid down. I took sixty out of the cashpoint yesterday, bought a sandwich at lunchtime. Apart from that, I haven't spent any—'

'Blimey,' he says. 'Kylie's talking about adopting twins!'

He turns the page. The waft sends a husk of spliff lolling across the ashtray, like a relic from a mummy's tomb.

'So have you, then?'

Finally he looks up. His eyes have that arch, pot-hazed insolence I have come to dread.

'*How d'you mean?*' he repeats with scornful exasperation.

Existential philosophy isn't Anthony's thing, so it is safe to assume he's buying time. The spending spree is short.

'Why do you always do this, Dan?' he snaps.

Whenever he counters a question with a question, I've got my answer. I take a breath.

'Why do I always do what, Anthony?'

'Go on about how much *fucking money* you've got!'

And that's when I get that powerless feeling …

'Erm, I'm actually going on about how much money I haven't got ...'

It's like being a foxhound, trapped at the dead centre of the pack.

'You know I'm having a shit time,' he sneers, 'but you've always got to rub it in – haven't you?'

You alone spot the fox, chortling behind a tree stump.

'Anthony, this isn't a big deal, all I want to know is—'

Try and go after it … Just as the momentum of a hundred bodies impels you in the opposite direction.

Anthony's fist hits the table.

Too late. The fox is away.

'You come back every night, rattling on about fucking Javelin! You know it winds me up, after the way they shafted me …' Revising history is one of Anthony's things. 'And when you're not doing that, you're waving your big, fat fucking salary in my face!'

Suddenly he's up from the table, face magma red, an inch from mine. His mouth is a hard line as he spits: 'Get out the way! *You make me want to puke!*'

His palm strikes my shoulder. It's a shove, not a

punch, but enough to sting. I lose my footing – and I'm twisting backwards, over the glass panels of the door lying on the tiles ... In a slow-motion moment, my first instinct is to break the fall. My outstretched hand crashes through the brittle pane, taking my body weight as the glass shatters in a burst of sugary splinters.

For a second, I feel nothing. I can't bring myself to look. Then the burning sensation begins, seeping up my wrist like snake venom. As I lift my hand from the shards, Anthony is kneeling beside me, pushing the shirtsleeve up my arm.

'Can you move it?'

I can, but I still don't want to see it. He's casting round the kitchen, for something to clean it with, or maybe the phone to call for help. Whatever it is, he can't find it.

Looking back, it's hard to say which hurt more: the cuts or his voice, drifting down the hall.

'Get up, you big girl – it's only a scratch. Where did I put my spliff?'

*

That was a landmark. Not because it was the last row we ever had, but because it's when the twitching started.

Duncan has explained it, though I've never followed the full neuro-logic. Somehow, the nerve damage I sustained as I hit the deck is the root of the slight but relentless twitch in my left arm, shoulder and eye. It comes on whenever I'm nervous or run-down.

The cuts needed stitches, leaving a scar exactly one

centimetre from the artery. Before it had a chance to fade, previously unfathomable things became clear. How battered wives can grit their teeth and live in denial; how murderers evade arrest because their spouse keeps schtum. If you want someone badly enough, you'll forgive them anything. And at that stage in my life, gravitating from one half-arsed stab at a relationship to another, I didn't want to fail again. No other man I'd ever met made me think: *This is it. If I never sleep with anyone else, then fine …*

And if love is blind, lust is blinder. Because, from the curl of his arrogant lip to the curve of his peachy arse, Anthony James Duke had the X factor – and what an insidious drug that is! I forgave him what happened that night. After all, like he said, an accident's an accident.

It made no difference. A few days later, money disappeared again, so I started hiding my wallet. Then he started reading my diary – to my mind the ultimate invasion of privacy. People write diaries for different reasons; mine fulfilled the role of occasional therapist. When the going was good, I would neglect it for months, returning abruptly when in need of solace. Lately, I had never needed it more. Entries were short – frenzied scribblings I made when Anthony was in the shower, or out at the shops. So to realise he was reading it was like waking up and finding him crouched inside my head.

From then on, I kept my diary at work. But this was the last straw. The more I knew him, the less I liked him. I realised what he wanted was the cosy infrastructure of a relationship – the nice little flat, the social ease of a presentable bloke at his side – with none of the daily grind, and as little as possible of the nightly.

Anthony didn't screw around. He didn't beat me up, or hide bodies under the floorboards. But he made me feel afraid in my own home. The rows became more frequent, his reasoning more intractable. I told him to get out, not once but twice – the first time asking him back a day later, with an illogicality that made me hate myself. In the quick-time pace that epitomised our relationship, we reunited, rekindled, made love, ate pizza, rowed and parted again, in the space of an afternoon.

Still I wasn't sure.

'I can cancel the cab,' I said as we waited in silence by the front door.

'Fuck you, Dan,' he said.

As he tossed back my keys there were tears in his eyes that might have been his or another fearsome beast's.

Either way, I never saw him again.

CHAPTER TWENTY-FOUR

It's a Saturday afternoon when I get the text from Duncan.

> MEET ME AT BARREL 9.30. SOMETHING
> TO CELEBRATE. D X

Despite not having to worry about the drudgery of going to work with a hangover, tonight is only my second visit to our local gay bar since the falling of the beautiful axe. It's not that I've been abstaining from alcohol; more that you can't beat a laptop and a four-pack when you're trawling for a six-pack.

Luckily for the management at the Barrel, their regulars are less reclusive. By all accounts they've had a cracking summer, helped by the fine weather and their French doors that open onto the pavement. The trestle tables outside are always thronging when I pass, as they are tonight.

I'm half an hour early, but that's okay. I became immune to the awkwardness of standing in a bar on my own years ago ... The Barrel & Tap is depressingly – or comfortingly, depending on your mood – like a thousand boys' bars on the planet: music videos on multiple screens, a neon-lit bar, and clientele that span the social strata from underage scallywags to the suited-and-booted. I'd swear that, when they finished at the Jobcentre Plus, the same interior design team nipped round the corner to their next project ... The floor is divided into an unnecessary number of levels: there's a sunken mezzanine here, a dais there, giving a variety of vantage points and perspectives.

There's a balcony too, above the bar. That's where I wait for Duncan, sipping my beer and trying not to blink too much. Unusually, one of the sofas is free; but they're saggier than they look, so when you sit your hips sink to ankle level till you're peering through your knees. For an unimpeded view of the door, I stand at the railing instead, watching the blobs of light from the glitter ball whirl around the ceiling.

Even with five barmen on, the service here is hopeless. They look cute in their matching T-shirts; one in particular, with fuzzy forearms and biceps so worked they have corners. He's got good shoulders, speaks with an Aussie twang and you can just see him shearing a sheep. Not normally my thing – but I'm thinking it could be sexy if he's doing it, just as Duncan's ready-shorn head comes bobbing through the crowd. He winks up at me, then waits to be served. A lengthy process, during which he also clocks the Aussie, and is sufficiently impressed to hang back till he's caught his eye.

Unfaithful to his Scottish roots, Duncan is the most generous person I know, so I finish my beer in anticipation of another. But, after conferring with the barman and an appearance by his credit card, he bounds up the stairs with an ice bucket and two champagne flutes.

'Aw, wasn't it worth the wait to see his wrist action with that cork?' he says, handing me the glasses while he pours.

'Don't tell me – you've had your offer accepted on a flat!'

Dunc smiles. 'Close ...' He waits for the bubbles to subside before topping us up. 'The good news is: Colin's transferred the fifty grand, so I can make an offer tomorrow. I'm in the money, babe! Briefly …'

He is positively glowing with excitement. Living under the same roof as his ex has been tricky for them both. They've been commendably mature since they split up eighteen months ago. But sorting out the finances has been a strain, and it hasn't been easy drawing an emotional line under their relationship as they stood over the same toaster each morning.

'Congratulations, Dunc! Here's to new beginnings. You deserve it.'

'I can't believe it,' he says, running fingertips over his stubbly scalp. 'My own place, at last. I'll be able to shag at home whenever I like, not just when he's away!'

Judging by his recent texts, their domestic set-up has been a hindrance to his sex life like a kerbstone to a tsunami. Colin is away on business every other week, and Duncan thrives on five hours' sleep. He thinks nothing of hooking up for something kinky in Braintree at half-eleven, then driving off into the night. God knows what he'll get up to now.

The Barrel's house bubbly has the price tag of a decent vintage, if not the taste. But after two or three sips, it's slipping down nicely.

'So, which property are you going for?' I ask. I've lost track of what's in the running.

'A fab one-bed flat in Clapham Old Town. Ground-floor Victorian conversion, own garden. Backs onto the railway line – but you know me, I could sleep through the Charge of the Light Brigade if it wasn't for the uniforms ...'

As we finish the bottle, I have to restrain him from buying another. He's on even better form than usual and I can see the relief in his eyes. The Barrel has a late licence at weekends, and within an hour you can hardly move. Posters announce a Janet Jackson 2-4-1 Crush Bar, which means mayhem and an even longer wait at the bar when one of her tracks skitters through the speakers. I can tell Dunc is looking to consummate his good fortune; he is fumbling in the pocket of his boot-cut jeans, giving any new arrival with an even number of limbs his full appraisal.

'My spuds are like space-hoppers,' he says, 'let's go downstairs … ' He leads the way, the better to immerse himself in the possibilities.

We find ourselves a nook between the cigarette machine and the cloakroom that doubles as the VJ's control booth. The top of the vending machine is thoughtfully contoured so that resting glasses slide straight to the floor. We keep hold of ours and chance the sea of jogging elbows. Beside me is a lad with a badger hairdo; he is imperiously camp with springy buttocks. His red and green T-shirt features a Welsh dragon with a suggestive tongue and the caption *BOYO-HAZARD*. He is capering away in a fair approximation of vogueing, despite the fact he was surely in nappies when Madonna introduced the dance to the world. I feel like telling him I could do all that first time round. But I don't, because we are studiously ignoring each other, and because it's a lie.

All around us, bolstered by alcohol or whatever, well-honed bodies are losing their reserve. Assignations are made as the corners of mouths weaken into smiles. Even the genetically unblessed are finding their confidence.

Duncan is chatting up a tallish man with the build of a games teacher and the hairstyle of my old physics mistress. He is wearing jeans and a too-tight cycling top with a zipper at the neck. Gay men have a way of being the first to embrace a fashion, and the last to let it go. Then I notice his nipple rings, conspicuous as polo mints through the fabric. Duncan can spot a piercing at thirty paces and they drive him wild. Part of me wishes I was as easily stirred as he is, instead of standing here picking holes in people, trying to keep my left eyebrow quiet.

Mr Cycle Top disappears to get change for cigarettes and gives Duncan's bum an appreciative squeeze on the way.

'Name's Eric,' says Dunc with a grin. 'Solicitor. Lives in Forest Hill. He's going to the Vauxhall – do you fancy it?'

The Vauxhall Arms is famous for its Saturday-night drag acts and the most insanitary toilets since the Mary Rose. Not my favourite venue, but fun on a good night.

'Who's on?'

'Millicent Tendency, Eric says. Come on, you know it cheers you up seeing grown men cry …'

Millicent Tendency, the self-styled 'Disco-Bunny Boiler of London Town', is famous for her audience humiliation. Her act is set in stone: the same old mantra of dirty jokes and musical interludes. She's been alternating Saturday nights at the Vauxhall with Honey Lingus, 'The Irish Bond Girl', for as long as anyone can remember. It's earned her an ardent following, and there's something perversely comforting about her flick-knife delivery.

If I say I don't want to go, Duncan will knock back his beau rather than leave me on my own. But I don't feel like spoiling his fun.

'Go on,' I say. 'I'll just have a pee first …'

Both cubicles in the ladies are full, so I try the gents. There's a queue in there too, with three of us waiting for the only stall. For someone who's had his tackle appraised by more men than Roy Keane, I've never been good with urinals. That said, I'm nearly desperate enough to chance it.

I'm trying to take my mind off my bladder, by reading a poster about a pick-up service for pissheads that sends a man on a Meccano scooter to drive you home in your own car. Just then, the cubicle door opens – and out troop Jack, Phil and … nobody. This is the first time I've seen them since we got the tube home in silence from Heathrow Airport.

They look as surprised as I am; thrown for a second, like I rumbled them doing something they shouldn't. They catch me checking for a third party in the cubicle and Jack, at least, smiles. I can't see them still being so horny for each other they'd do it standing up in a toilet, so that only leaves illegal substances or a plumbing thesis.

'Hi, fella,' says Jack, his cheeky cheeks even more pinchably flushed than usual.

'Dan,' nods Phil from inside the washbasin mirror. His eyes are as cold as the glass.

'Hello, Boys … Making a night of it?'

Jack hesitates, unsure if it's safe to touch my arm or peck me on the cheek.

'We're off to the Exodus later,' says Phil.

From his tone, this is not an invitation. The Exodus is more trippy and less rubbery than the clubs they used to frequent. Perhaps The Boys have moved on in more ways than one.

'How about you?' asks Jack, as Phil snaps the roller towel to the dry side.

'I'm out with Dunc. We're off in a minute.'

The cubicle comes free again. The guy in front of me has succumbed to the trough, so it's my turn.

'Have fun,' says Phil on his way out.

'Yeah, have fun,' says Jack, like he means it. We pause in our respective doors like Mr and Mrs Weatherman and both risk half a smile.

I shunt the toilet door a mite harder than it requires. I'm locked in behind the chipboard partition, with the smell of piss and the throb of Janet Jackson's 'Rhythm Nation'. And I wonder what the fuck I'm doing with my life.

I am forty in less than a month. That's four-zero … I can remember hanging out in bars like this when I was twenty, then thirty, thinking: *Not long now – I'll meet the right guy soon* … Then I got into the being-single thing, and my thirties proved as dirty as everyone said. But, right now, I feel kinship with that clapped-out old slapper in the song: you know, the one who'd been undressed by kings and seen things a woman's not supposed to … Not any actual kings in my case, unless you count Aaron Shadwick. But I've sleazed my way through enough risqué scenarios in the last few years to put Jack and Phil at the respectable end of the market. And I'm not at all sure why.

I finish peeing and lean against the tiles, one foot joggling on a bubble in the lino. The more I think about it, the more I see that Anthony is where it went horribly wrong. I never trusted anyone after him. I never wanted to.

God, listen to me … You'd think he broke both my

legs and strangled my pet hamster. When all he really did was screw me up so badly, the only men I connect with are quick, gratuitous fucks and other people's boyfriends. If anyone shows a genuine interest, I either run a mile or pull them apart in my head before they get a chance.

Tart, yes. Commitment phobe, definitely. Terminally damaged emotional fuck-up? Maybe.

But, hey, if this is how I want to live my life, so be it. With a fair wind and a vat of moisturiser, I've got another ten years while my looks hold together enough to be desirable in this fickle world. After that, it's witty-old-queen-in-the-corner time; with even more porn and possibly rent boys.

Dan, only you can decide …

The queue has gone when I unlock the cubicle. Just a solitary guy at the trough. It's the sheep shearer.

Knob ogling is crass in the extreme; I think we can all agree on that. But as I rinse my hands it's hard not to sneak a peek, and in a place like this it's practically de rigueur. It doesn't risk you a head-butt, as it would in a straight pub, which is one of the ways gay bars differ. You don't find pubes in the urinals here, either. Gay men are inveterate trimmers, and pubic hairs are like hot-air balloonists: the shorter they are, the less they fall out.

The other difference is, gay men can take an entire pee without gobbing in the trough. Straight men find this impossible, though one does wish they'd try.

'Haawwk-*tuuh!*' flobs the Aussie, before a bouncy shake-and-button-up.

That's another thing about men as cute as he is. They're always too good to be true.

187

CHAPTER TWENTY-FIVE

The following Thursday, I'm in the West End. Sweating.

Following an email tip-off from Gina, I've wangled two freebies for the opening night of Brenda Allen's one-woman show. Brenda Allen was in *The Sunshine Girls*, a geriatric precursor to *Sex and the City*, from the days when American sitcoms were still coy as a carp; all sharp one-liners and innuendos, minus the references to clitoral stimulation.

The waspish wit of *The Sunshine Girls* made it a big hit with the brotherhood – and – surprise, surprise – they're out in force tonight. I'm waiting under the theatre awning for Sandra, who's got a green card from her husband. It's the first time I've seen her in weeks; her family life abhors a vacuum, and since she's given up work a never-ending round of school runs, scout meetings, judo and fencing lessons have expanded to fill it.

It is ten minutes to curtain-up before she and her enormous handbag scurry into view. She's wearing a purple, crushed-velvet top and black pedal pushers. And, like me, she is glowing.

''Allo, love,' she says with a peck. 'Too hot to get ponced up for a premiere, innit?'

'Tell me about it. This is the first time I've had trousers on in months.'

She laughs dirtily. 'Still on the net, then.'

'I mean *long* trousers, you minx. I'm on a bigger belt hole too, dammit.' Nothing lulls you into a false sense of midriff security like a summer in elasticated waists. 'Come on,' I say. 'Let's find our seats …'

We squeeze through the foyer, which is mobbed with a mix of oldies in evening wear and not-so-smart casuals. A notice taped to the box office says TONIGHT – SOLD OUT, and from behind the window a girl with ginger hair and matching glasses is talking to a pair of flushed Americans.

Struggling through the smoky little bar we take our seats in the stalls. Row F, smack in the middle. Good old Gina and her box-office mafia.

'Bloody 'ell,' says Sandra, popping up from stowing her bag under the seat. 'That's whats-'er-name!'

She's right, it is. In fact, the whole place is B-list central, with a goodly smattering of soap stars and TV presenters taking their places beside the A-list gays. *The Sunshine Girls* is the kind of show gay men of a certain age have in a box set at the back of the cupboard. Not regular viewing, but a good standby for a nostalgic chortle.

When the chimes go and a voice announces two minutes to showtime, two-thirds of the seats are still empty. It is see-and-be-seen night, so the in-crowd cling to the bar till the bitter end. At five-past-curtain they're still milling in through the side doors, meeting the programme-sellers' cajoling with glazed indifference.

'Look at 'im!' whispers Sandra. She's in her element, swivelling like a weathercock. I follow her eyebrows to the row behind. The man taking his seat is a game-show host and old-school raconteur, here with his Thai ex-beauty-queen wife. They're both dolled up like Oscars night, but it's hard to get a decent look when they're right behind us.

We're under starter's orders. The hubbub is dying down when a last grande dame makes her entrance. She is late-sixties and walks with a stick; has that Hampstead look – artisanal poncho, big belt – accessorised with a grungy youth in arse-crack jeans, who I hope to God is her grandson. She hobbles gamely from one side of the auditorium to the other via the foot of the stage ... I know I know her, but I can't get the name. She looks like a Redgrave but isn't, and I wish Gina was here. She always knows everyone.

'Who's that, Sand?'

Sandra cranes her neck, following their progress up the aisle. The great lady is avoiding gazes, looking indulgently at the gum-spotted carpet.

'Dunno,' she says as the lights go down. 'I think he's in a boy band ...'

Out of the gloom, a stentorian voice booms: 'Ladeez and gennelmen! Put your hands together for the Boston Bombshell – *Miss* – *Brenda* – *Allen*!'

The audience erupts in a frenzy of whooping as the star of the show glides into the spotlight in her signature sequined housecoat. Brenda at eighty looks like Brenda at sixty: a testament to healthy living, surgery or petrification. She's six-foot-plus in heels, hair frothy white and eyes mouthwash blue – the spitting image of one of the dead Doctor Whos—

'Why, thank you, and good evening!'

—except her voice is deeper. Brenda Allen is one of a dying breed of troupers. After a lifetime of vaudeville and bit parts, she finally made it big with *The Sunshine Girls*. On its first run I was at school, and she was what they called 'a comedienne'; a term I find strangely ambivalent to this day. Apposite in her case, because, with her statuesque build, gravelly voice and voluminous gowns, rumours abounded there was more to Brenda Allen than met the eye. It was the sort of scurrilousness that amused my schoolmates no end. And me; although, coinciding as it did with my own gender-based dilemma, my laughter tended to peter out first. One day, Eddie Sanderson brought in a feature from the *Sunday People*. About Brenda Allen reversing a Chevy over her own grandchild as she pulled out of the gas station (*Grandchild! Then she must have had kids!*) And so, with perverse pubescent logic, those rumours were laid to rest.

This show, her first in London for a decade, is a saucy but sanitised retread of her life in showbiz. She tells a few gags, sings a few songs; all accompanied by her 'oldest, dearest friend – Morgan Goldbloom!' He sits at the back of the stage at an ebony baby grand, acting the straight guy and occasional prompt with a face as crumpled as a hurriedly shed sock. The supportive crowd soaks it up. The celebs applaud respectfully, nodding and rolling their eyes in empathy at the mention of anyone famous. Her gay fan base picks up on all the references to the TV show, firing back lines from classic episodes across the footlights. Like the one where Brenda and chums are trapped in the elevator, and play themselves as teens in the flashbacks.

Sandra never watched it, and she's getting restless after one too many in-jokes and Broadway standards. As the lights come up at the interval, she sparks back to life.

'Gawd, they love her, don't they? If I give you some money, will you get us an ice cream?'

191

'Don't you fancy a drink?'

'Nah,' she says, scrabbling for her purse. 'I promised Lizzie I wouldn't smoke today. She found a big, black fungus on our horse chestnut. Stuck my photo in it and left it on the step. "Look, Mummy," she says, "that's what your lungs look like …"'

The air con is non-existent, so there's a major run on ice creams. I queue up behind a guy called Jed, who came third in the last series of *Big Brother*. His shirt is filmy linen and fitted to corset-tightness. It's gone sweatily transparent where the small of his back has pressed into the seat. A Celtic shield tattoo peeps over his waistband, like the sun rising out of what I and four million other viewers can confirm is a very toothsome arse. He asks for two tubs of strawberry, then realises he forgot his wallet. Given his status tonight, straddling both A- and B-lists, he shows a remarkable lack of embarrassment as he semaphores a mate for cash.

I pick my way back to the seat. Sandra is pretending to apply make-up while studying Mr and Mrs Game Show in her compact. They have also eschewed the bar, magicking ice creams from somewhere. I make heavy work of clambering past knees to get a decent look. Mrs Game Show's hair is as immaculate as her strappy black dress; her arms are aubergine firm, and free of the dinner-lady heftiness that is the curse of women her age. She eats her ice cream slowly, with a sensuousness even I find mildly arousing. I'm reminded of a peasant girl in an ad for pasta sauce I fixated on as a child; she had the same naïve beauty as Mrs Game Show, and knockers bursting out of her blouse in a manner not unlike Jed's … Mr Game Show is immaculate, too. He wears a tux and a look of disdain, perhaps at the way theatre crowds don't dress up any more. He's the exact same shade as his wife, though he's Home Counties through and through. Seventy if he's a day, his face is like a walnut that time and sand have chafed to a wrinkle-free sheen. Famously, he's also wearing something else.

'Tell you what,' whispers Sandra, as I slip her something creamy and a plastic spoon, 'it's a bloody good rug ...'

'Put that mirror away!' I hiss. 'They could have bodyguards for all you know.'

'I'm only looking!' she snips, snapping her compact. She peels the lid off her ice cream and licks it.

'Now, I'm telling you this now...' Her voice has the brisk tone that always sent a shudder through me at work; the one her kids hear when they're about to get a bollocking. 'Dave and I have been talking – and we've decided, come September, I've got no choice but to get a job. The school fees are up again, and Frank's year are going to Peru for the Inca whatnots, and he's dying to go.'

'Peru? With the school? We were lucky to get Snowdonia!'

'I know. Costs a bleeding arm and a leg ... Anyway, no pressure, but even if I do it on me tod, I'm gonna have to put feelers out. Phone round Shelley Pembridge and that lot.' She takes another scoop of ice cream. 'Have you given it any more thought?'

I stop chewing. The last glob of strawberry slips down unassisted.

'Not really, Sand. I keep telling myself I'll think about it after my birthday. Ask me again in a month. I see your point, though – a girl's gotta do what a girl's gotta do.'

'Cheers,' she says. 'We'll talk after your party. You are still having one, yeah? First Saturday of the month?'

That's a point. 'God – time I did something about that. I'll do an email when I get home.' The bell chimes for the end of the interval. 'Hang on, I just need to ...'

It's a lifestyle-defining condition, having a bladder the size of an ant's handbag. I shuffle to the other end of the row this time, to avoid being tutted by the same people twice. And that's when I see Martin, striding smartly down the aisle ... I don't remember how we met, but he and I had a fling years ago. Actually, it was a series of flings, culminating in a weekend at his house in Dorset. One of those episodes you realise you've excised from memory till it pops up unannounced. All I remember about Dorset is an impractical bed on castors, and not really fancying him when it came to it. In Martin's eyes, I think that weekend was my final audition for the role of boyfriend. I didn't pass; in fact, I don't think we ever saw each other again. Presumably I sank into his mire of forgotten conquests as quickly as he did into mine.

'*Dan!*' says Martin with a contrived smile.

At least we remember names. We walk down the velvet-walled corridor, presumably with the same destination in mind.

'Quite a night,' I say, fumbling for small talk. 'All these celebrities ... Trouble is, I can never remember who's who.'

'Oh,' says Martin, tossing his jaw like a land-owning stud in a Brontë adaptation. 'Does it *really* matter?'

The bell goes again as we reach the toilets.

Martin is an actor. He's never made it.

*

When I get home, I go on the net. Send Gina a quick thank-you for the tickets. I'm just trying to think of a witty, original way to couch my party invitation, when up pops a reply. I'm surprised to see her online at this time of night. It's always possible she is cruising for throbbing man-cock, but probably not.

> *Glad you enjoyed the show. Thought it more you than me. Oh, and while I'm doing my fairy godmother bit, how do you fancy a free trip to Italy?*

CHAPTER TWENTY-SIX

At 11.30 a.m. the following Thursday, I should be signing on. But Viv at the Jobcentre Plus has given me a dispensation to visit my second cousins in Arbroath. Apparently even the downtrodden get a holiday, and the dole still pays out if you're 'available for work'. That means not leaving the country; hence the fabricated relatives in Arbroath, which sounds like a convincing mobile-signal blackspot to me. It's my cover story, on the off-chance Viv comes up with something six-figured-and-fabulous at Saatchis while I'm in Italy; between calls to her daughter about knitting and who shut the cat in the airing cupboard.

So instead, I'm staring down at the cloud. A great big rolling ice floe of it, stretching all the way to a faux horizon. This bit looks like the remnants of a snow fight; over there, a rocky outcrop, so solid you wouldn't blink if a sled and huskies skimmed into view at any moment.

Gina is asleep. She can do that on planes, though she said she wouldn't this time. It's the conference documents that did it. I lift them gently off her lap and slip them in the seat pocket. Livid as I am that I left my new *Doctor Who Magazine* in the bathroom, I'm not sufficiently bored to flick through *The Cross-Cultural Interface in the Context of Independent Drama – Trieste, 11–14 August*.

You can tell Gina's work is publicly funded because we're flying budget. Suits me; it's the only bit I'm paying for. The theatre is picking up the tab for the transfers, and the accommodation which, according to the website, is smack in the middle of town with glorious sea views ... God bless tonsils, that's what I say. If her boss's kid wasn't under the knife tomorrow, neither of us would be here.

Tell you the truth, I feel slightly comforted to be travelling Ryanair these days. If I was a terrorist seeking immortality, I'd want to take down more than a crateful of tabloid-token-cutters. What I don't like is the dehydration, which I'm doing my best to pre-empt by downing a litre of water. The plastic bottle is too fat for the elasticated pocket, so it's between my thighs, buckling forlornly under the cabin pressure like a balloon animal after a birthday party.

'Sandwich?' says Dean, with his costermonger's spread and a glint in his eye that implies we are brightening each other's day.

'I'm fine, thanks,' I say – like we don't both know it.

The seatbelt sign bongs and my bottle starts to tense. We're preparing to land.

'Going down, Dan?' says Gina, jolting back to life.

Like I say, she doesn't miss a thing.

*

Trieste Airport is as small as you'd expect. Just a couple of sorry shops selling souvenirs of Venice, which implies there may be even less to Trieste itself than I fear.

Our driver is there to meet us. I'm quite jealous of Gina, because having your name spelt wrong on a big piece of cardboard is definitely something you're meant to do before you're forty. The driver is small, with hair like iron filings. He hoists our holdalls from trolley to boot with an ease that suggests I ought to eat more pasta.

As we drive into the city, Gina's body language is making me feel guilty. Mine says 'Carefree holiday slob'; hers says 'Businesswoman en route to important meeting'.

'You'll be free in the evenings, though, won't you?' I ask considerately.

'Too right,' she says. 'I told Beth, I'm only doing this if I can bring someone and wriggle out of the socialising. Did my research yesterday – there's a trattoria that does nice things with truffles, round the corner from the hotel …'

We follow the curve of the coast road, with the Adriatic to starboard and Huey Lewis on the radio. Out on the water, strings of white floats nod like line-dancing seagulls. It's funny but, wherever I am in the world, when I see the sea I always remember the last time. In this case, it was the cold grey Baltic, as I cabbed it back to Helsinki airport with The Boys. Here, the water is the safe blue of a long-ago family holiday, when a pretty little girl with a chest as flat as mine and a sunhat on elastic taught me to count to *dix*.

Lonely homes and prefabs give way to the grid, as we skip the outskirts and enter the city. Trieste reminds me of Liverpool in unexpected sunshine. I will our driver to keep going until we reach a quarter more in keeping with my idea of an Italian city. It's to no avail; he pulls up in a narrow street perpendicular to the sea, which looks lamentably like Bootle.

'Here you go,' says Gina, tipping the man in euros.

I follow her out of the cab, stepping into sunshine more searing than we left at home.

*

'Phew,' she says, whipping off the bedspread. 'Bet you thought your luck was in!'

The mattresses fit together so matily, the difference between two singles and a double is the linen alone; the individual duvets and bottom sheets reveal we're the proud custodians of twins.

We start to unpack, which will take a minute in my case. I'm travelling light. So is Gina, though I see she has also packed a couple of slinky numbers.

'Got time to go walkabout?' I say, spotting a map slipped into the desk-top blotter. 'Looks like we're round the corner from some big square ...'

She commandeers the best hangers, leaving me the chicken wire.

'Wish I could. Got a meet-and-greet at four, but if I show my face there I reckon I can cry off dinner. Why don't you have a scout round, book us a table somewhere?'

She showers, changes into something more businesslike than her Muji track pants, and goes in search of her fellow delegates. The conference is at the hotel, and with the time difference it isn't long to kick-off.

While she's gone, I flick through the satellite for porn. I think I've found some, but it turns out to be a glam Italian soap. The lip liner and pneumatic bosoms don't signify girl-on-girl action, after all – or not that kind ... There's a brief, guttural spat with much pointing of polished nails, then the blonde and brunette launch into the obligatory catfight. The blonde tumbles down a flight of stairs and immediately miscarries in her leather trousers. Even if my Italian wasn't up to '*A-iiii! Mio bambino!*' the hand clutching her stomach and avalanche of glycerine tears speak for themselves.

The scene cuts to a tight shot of a man in a Hawaiian shirt. He is lounging on a beach we are supposed to believe is tropical, judging by the parlour palms. I flick to the Italian shopping channel, where two presenters extol the virtues of a rubber storage bag. It has an attachment that sucks out the air for reasons of spatial economy. They demonstrate this on a hapless teddy bear, which is instantly mummified in the same way as a man in Hackney I've seen on click4dick,

I put on shorts and flip-flops and slide the street map from its holder. On the back is a mosaic of ads, for local restaurants and designer discount stores. I slap on some factor 15 anywhere the sun might shine, and go off in search of supper.

*

The square I saw on the map is traffic-free and vast; big enough for polo, if you could trust the horses not to run into the statues. It's fringed with cafés on three sides and the fourth looks out to sea. At the tables, stylish men and women are doing the Italian thing, lunching into the afternoon; waiters stride about with trays, clearing up the debris without a hint of servility.

I'm not hungry after two in-flight sandwiches, so I buy another bottle of water at the newsstand and head away from the sea. Beyond the major thoroughfares there are few people around. I find myself up a steep, narrow alley. It turns pleasingly cobbled halfway up, cooler in the shadows and dark enough to make my sunglasses a tripping hazard. With a toothless granny on a doorstep here, or a window basket there, it could be anywhere in the Mediterranean. Instead, it's deserted – a soulless place of locked doors and windows shuttered to the sun.

The gradient rises as I round the bend, to a clang of machinery and a very different scene. Behind the façade of the narrow street, an earth mover is rending masonry to dust like a daffodil-yellow Godzilla. A white van with three hard hats on the bonnet is parked up beside the devastation. Behind the windscreen, the radio is tuned to football and three young men are eating bread rolls. Their eyes follow me as I cross the road, in a way that could be threatening or quite a thrill. But they're Italian; that's just what they do.

I look at the map and meander on through streets and more streets, all of which would be peaceful if not for the cacophony of construction. For now, I've slipped into Building Site World – where every corner is dusty and scaffolded, and the natives are warriors in filthy boots with roaring, obedient machines. One thirty-foot monster is asleep at the end of another street, toothed head furled to the ground in a yoga pose. Then I'm out of this other dimension as swiftly as I arrived: onto Via Felice Venzian, where there should be a nice-looking bistro, just right for us tonight. According to the advert, a burnished copper swordfish hangs on chains over the door and they serve the city's finest seafood.

Yep, there it is – between the grocer's and a travel agent.

It isn't open, but I try to decipher the fish dishes on the menu from any Latin names I recall from my youth as a natural-history geek. Except I only remember *Loxodonta africana*, and African elephant isn't on the menu. I can't see Gina eating bush meat, anyway – she's not that kind of girl – so this should be fine. I check the phone number is on the ad. And I'm just wondering whether to head home or dive back into Diggerville, when something utterly unexpected catches my eye.

I swear, if Babar himself had driven past on a hijacked forklift, I couldn't have been more surprised.

CHAPTER TWENTY-SEVEN

We never get to the restaurant. When I arrive back at the room, there's a note scribbled on a hotel envelope.

> *Sorry Dan*
> *Can't wriggle out of dinner after all. Good news*
> *(?) is I've wangled you a seat. Hotel restaurant*
> *8.30pm, table 16. Can you bear it?!*
> *G xx*

Damn. I was looking forward to a bit of gourmet seafood.

> *P.S. Theatre's paying.*

On the other hand, I did have tuna sandwiches earlier.

It strikes me I have precisely nothing to wear for a corporate dinner. If I want to keep my knees covered, my choice is a pair of jeans or sunblock. I opt for the former, teamed with my one long-sleeved shirt, which I wear untucked to cover a cheeky rip in the back of my Levi's.

I wander down to the bar, thinking I might be in time for an aperitif. But it's a big do, very regimented, and they've already been summoned to dine. The maitre d' runs a finger down his clipboard, then leads me to table sixteen with a withering glance at my trainers. Seven chairs are already taken, but there's an empty one next to Gina.

'I'm really sorry!' she says. 'We'll eat out tomorrow, I promise. Did you find somewhere nice?'

She's looking lovely in a black beaded top. And just a little flushed, which could be the wine.

'It'll keep,' I say, pouring myself a generous glass of white from the bottle on the table. 'How's the conference?'

'Oh, you know … Cheers!' She chinks my glass and looks away with a smile. And I have the tiniest suspicion there's something going on.

At this point, she's collared by an elegant lady in a long blue dress which whispers as she moves.

'Won't be a minute,' says Gina, doing her duty. The Italian lady leads her to another table at the far side of the salon. Two men in tuxes stand when they see her, losing their serviettes in their excitement. Both shake Gina's hand and one of them kisses it. The candlelight and heavy curtains give the scene a Renaissance air, and something of the stable lad about Gina's velvet slacks adds to the authenticity. The gentlemen chat effusively, making notes on their place cards; Gina nods and clasps her hands a lot.

'Do you think we need to rescue her?' says the guy one along from her empty chair. He's dressed like everyone else, though his collar button has already admitted defeat. 'You must be Dan … I'm Gareth.'

If this was Duncan we were talking about, pinpointing an ex-paramour would be like trying to spot a mate in the London Marathon. But with Gina's back catalogue, there aren't many to remember. In fact, in the time I've known her, there have been three; and unless I'm mistaken, this is one of them. Gareth worked for the Arts Council – something to do with funding. Gina and he had a clandestine thing the Christmas before last. A dinner here, a tumble there; I seem to remember a snatched weekend at a spa hotel, then it all went quiet. Gina never said much, but from what I could gather, Gareth's wife caught the whiff of extra-marital perfume and that was that ... Or so I thought. Eighteen months later, eight hundred miles away, here they are again.

'You're at this conference too, then?' I say, trying to keep the protective big-brother edge out of my voice.

'Just for a couple of days. I'm doing a presentation tomorrow – half of it in Italian, supposedly ...' The light glints off his wedding ring as he takes a swig of red. 'I'm bricking it.'

You know how you never think the people you really care about get the partners they deserve? Well, I'm glad there's still hope for Gina. There's nothing wrong with Gareth per se; he's just the regular kind of guy who cheats on his wife. Don't get me wrong, I think Gina's got the right idea; she doesn't judge men by their haircut, or whether they've got a six-pack – luckily for Gareth, because he doesn't even have a haircut. But I sometimes wonder how women and gay men evolved so differently ... Anthropologically, we share the same starting point (Being Single) and the same goal (Finding A Man); but then the rules diverge. Your metropolitan gay man will spend years foraging in the forest, taking a bite out of every shiny, exotic fruit he can lay his hands on then drop it to the floor; whereas women like Gina will weigh them up carefully, one at a time, open to the possibility of something gratifying beneath a less-than-perfect surface.

'Sorry about that,' says Gina, sitting back down. 'That was the chair and commissioning exec of a new 80 million euro arts complex in Milan. I promised Beth I'd schmooze them and slip them her email.' She catches my eyebrow. 'Dan, have you met Gareth?'

There's just time for a formal handshake before the hors d'oeuvres arrive – a mousse with a sprig of something green.

'Fancy you meeting him here,' I say innocently, as Gareth chats to the man on his other side.

'I had no idea, I swear!'

'Yeah? So when was the last time you, er … ?'

'God knows; must be eighteen months. He's not even at the Arts Council any more. Honestly, if I'd known he was coming, I'd—'

'Yeah, you wouldn't be sharing a room with me!'

She smiles and looks down at her plate. 'That's not the half of it. He's here with his brother …'

I'm lost. 'What did you have in mind – double date?'

'No. I mean, *he's* sharing a room too ...'

'A threesome? Go girl! Knew I could drag you down to my level eventually!'

She laughs. Then she sighs.

'Oh, well. C'est la vie.'

The other thing about women like Gina is, they can spend so long prodding and sniffing away at the peel, they get as disillusioned as the rest of us. And that's when they start to think the unthinkable. A romp with a married father-of-two takes on the same allure as a brawny skinhead waving his knob in the gents at John Lewis; one of those things you swore you'd never do till – oops, too late, you've done it.

Hand on heart, I honestly wish Gina could meet a nice guy even more than I wish it for myself. She's forty soon, too. And, call me old-fashioned, but it's still different for girls: a milestone for us, a millstone for them. And while she's on the trail, it's not like she has the easy, dial-a-ride route to carnal satisfaction I do. Sure, she could go on the net, but it doesn't appeal and I can't bring myself to encourage her. Not because she shouldn't have some fun, but because – well, I'd worry about her. And yeah, I *am* being a hypocrite and probably hetero-sexist. I'm sure ninety-nine per cent of the straight guys on there are fine. But what about the other one?

There is something rather sweet about the way they hold hands under the table between courses. And during courses, in the case of the pasta, which they manage with just forks. All so innocent, like the back row of the school bus – because, with circumstances as they are, they're stymied. I know for a fact the hotel's full, so barring a quick leg-over in the square, this is as far as their assignation is going tonight.

By the third glass of orvieto, even I can see Gareth has a certain charm. There's a twinkle about him; he doesn't bite his nails; and, let's face it, roadkill would look good in a tux ... Who am I to tell someone how to run their love life when I'm hardly making a great job of my own?

Hey – whatever gets you through the night.

I tap Gina's shoulder and whisper in her ear. Because I've just had an idea that could work out rather nicely for both of us.

CHAPTER TWENTY-EIGHT

It is an old-fashioned train with compartments. Like the ones in Agatha Christie, where buttoned-up types hide behind their newspapers, and little old ladies glint knowingly through their specs. Except I've got this one to myself; just me and the duffel bag I borrowed from Gina, lying in the net above my head. In fact the whole carriage looked pretty empty when I got on, bar a couple of backpackers and a mum with a trio of toddlers.

According to the timetable, the journey takes three hours. By my reckoning, that constitutes an hour and a half in motion and the same standing still. This is the second time we've ground to a halt – somewhere called Sežana, according to the platform sign. I saw two guards emerge from their breezeblock HQ about fifteen minutes ago. They'll be walking through the train, checking passports and looking surly if they're anything like the ones before the border.

The shorter one shows up at last, nodding curtly as he slides open the door. The epaulettes of his uniform say *Slovenska Mejna Policija*. It is brown crimplene, and not as flattering as the blue one being modelled an hour earlier. The Italian version looked like Armani might have had a hand in it and, truth to tell, I wouldn't have minded joining him.

'Where you go?' barks the border guard as I give him my passport.

'Ljubljana,' I reply, like he couldn't guess.

He finds an empty page and, to my delight, stamps it. They hardly ever do that these days.

'Why you go?'

'Holiday,' I say, as he hands it back.

But actually, that's a very good question.

*

It takes me a while to find the exit, but once I get out of the station, I'm on the main road into town.

The reception at our hotel had a leaflet in English about Ljubljana, which I read as I queued for my train ticket. Turns out that, like many cities, there's a river running through it. There's a castle on a hill too, and an Old Town which, according to the blurb, should not be missed. My return ticket is for 2.45 tomorrow afternoon. That gives Gina time for a night of passion and a long lie-in, before Gareth flies back to the nest via Stansted. It also gives me twenty-four hours to see the sights of the Slovenian capital.

I find a hotel just outside the Old Town, thinking it'll be cheaper than the historical heart. According to the girl on the desk, there's some sort of festival in town. They're nearly full up, so I take what she offers. The hotel is nothing special. Cookie-cutter three-star, with a bar that doubles as the breakfast room with a beige, fag-burned carpet.

My bedroom is quirkier. There's even a laminated song sheet in the ensuite. One side is in English and reads *Good morning! Slovenians love to sing in the shower!* followed by, unaccountably, the lyrics to 'Brown Girl in the Ring'. It'll look great in my bathroom, and it's the only thing worth nicking. The change of currency here also comes as a surprise. I need to find a cashpoint, or dinner will be the other half of my railway-station sandwich, toasted in the trouser press.

And that would be a real shame. Because I plan on eating out.

*

Getting back to the border guard's question: I'm here because I have no choice.

From the moment I saw that poster in the travel agent's window, my free will went on holiday. I hadn't the foggiest we were a hop and a skip from the Slovenian capital; I could no more direct you from Trieste to Ljubljana than Beijing to Bridlington.

I don't know what I want to say to Anthony, either. I'm not even sure I want to speak to him at all – but I would like to see him. Up close, in the flesh. See if I can tell what all the fuss was about; maybe exorcise a demon or two. And I want to see if he's changed – see if I was a necessary step in his rehab.

I stroll down to the Old Town, across the river. The Ljubljanica is narrower than the Thames but the waters are just as forbidding. The road that hugs the riverbank is alive with pedestrians, strolling in the sun. Like the buildings, the people here remind me of Prague: good-looking and chic-er than my post-Communist prejudice led me to expect.

I wander around for an hour, doing the whole of the Old Town but the castle. The hill is even steeper than it looked from the hotel, so I save it for the more forgiving morning sun. Eventually I reach the bridge that is enough of a landmark to make it onto all the postcards:

copper dragons at either end, wrapping arrow-headed tails around the stanchions. I squint up between the jaws of the nearest, to where a faraway wisp of cloud hovers like an exhalation.

I think it's high time I had a holiday drink, so I stop off at a bar for a beer. Cage birds twitter above the counter, but their song is being drowned by an extraordinary accordion version of something by Kraftwerk. Can you get any more European than that?

It is quarter past six and I haven't found anything approaching a 'gothic restaurant' yet. That was Tara's definition as I remember it, and it isn't much to go on. I thought if I wandered around long enough, I'd stumble across it. But the city is bigger than I expected, which leaves me the option of going home defeated or asking for help. Plenty of people seem to speak English, though that's not to say they are up to a word like 'gothic'. I can't think how to explain it without getting directed to the nearest graveyard.

Across the street there's a dusty-looking place with a window full of stickers for mobile-phone networks. Inside, figures are hunched over by the wall – salvation! I finish my beer, pay the man beneath the canaries, and leave Kraftwerk to their fate.

For 400 Slovenian tolars, I get half an hour on a tired old Dell – bags of time to track down a restaurant with a nifty bit of googling. But first I check my email. Then I can't resist a look at click4dick, just in case Matt Damon's been sifting the South London profiles for me again …

Only two messages, left soon after I was last online.

GR8GEEZER 00:57, August 11
ALLO MATE. HOT INNIT. WAS UP YOUR
NECK OF THE WOODS TODAY, DOWN
TOOTING LIDO. SHAME YOU WEREN'T
THERE IN YOUR SWIMMIES **GRIN**
WHEN WE HAVING THAT BEER.

MALCANDEDWIN 01:12, August 11
Two cute guys in Kennington, 26 and 41, in the
mood to party. Looking for third for fun this
weekend. Hot, drug-free session, optional
bondage, own dungeon. Check us out why don't
you?
[1] [2] [3] [4] [5]

Picture [1] is more than sufficient ... I'm about to log off when another message pops up.

MAESTROMAN 18:47, August 13
Hi Dan. Not out in the sunshine? Guess you
can have too much of a good thing.

I tap out a quick reply.

HORNYDSW4 18:47, August 13
afternoon maestro. actually it's rapidly
approaching evening here. i'm in ljubljana, would
u believe, looking for somewhere to go tonight.

MAESTROMAN 18:49, August 13
Fancy. What on earth takes you there? Want me
to look up Ljubljana in Spartacus, find you a
raunchy bar?!

Spartacus is the three-inch-thick guide to the gay establishments of the world. It is reprinted every year and almost every homo has one, even though it's perennially out of date and the inaccuracy of its maps is legendary. I once spent two hours traipsing round the wrong part of Paris because they'd omitted an entire arrondissement. I've not bought one since, though I do sometimes borrow Duncan's. He collects every edition religiously and calls it 'Spurticus', which doesn't tell you anything you don't already know.

> *HORNYDSW4 18:51, August 13*
> *don't think so thanks. can stay home and get*
> *raunchy bars. plus i always end up snagging*
> *my watch winder on the camouflage netting.*
> *i'm after some funny goth restaurant, as it*
> *happens … anyway, got to whizz, i'm on a*
> *timer in a net caff. catch up next week. xxx*

Typing 'Ljubljana restaurants' into Google brings up pages of possibilities. I click a link to a site where punters have left reviews for what seems like every eaterie in town. It looks promising, so I scroll down …

I have high hopes for a place called 'Hot Horse', though it turns out to be a burger bar selling something you don't even get in McDonald's. Most of the other names are in Slovenian, which means they're either short and sound like swear words, or long with a lot of Zs and not many vowels.

I'm on the last page, about to give up the ghost – when, appropriately, up pops 'Rico The Happy Skeleton'. The reviewer, who goes by the name of

HEYBOB80, rates it 'great for a night out but there's only four tables, so take your buddies and swamp it!!' I suspect HEYBOB80 is a bit of a lush, since he doesn't mention the food at all, though he's impressed by the wine list. He didn't have a camera handy, either, since the space for a pic says *No Photo Available.* Nothing for me to scrutinise for a glimpse of a tasty blue-eyed devil skulking in the background, tea towel over one arm. Nonetheless, HEYBOB80 mentions the 'freaky atmosphere', and he bets 'this place kicks ass on Hallowein!!' (sic).

Which is enough to tell me that 'Rico The Happy Skeleton' is where I'll be eating tonight.

CHAPTER TWENTY-NINE

In another hour it is almost dark. The temperature has dropped and it might even rain. I find the place easily enough. It's just off a street called Stari trg.

The door is down an alley, a sort of tunnel joining parallel streets. I'm pleased to see it's not in a part of town I scoped out earlier; that hand-painted sign, with its row of plastic skulls knocking together like coconuts, would take a bit of missing.

The restaurant is shut, and I'm sensing a pattern here. A postcard pinned to the door says it opens at nine. I consider staking it out until then, but music is coming from somewhere and I spot the adjacent staircase. It's presumably part of the same establishment, judging by the assorted animal skeletons lining the walls as I descend. There's a floor-to-ceiling bookcase of antique volumes at the turn in the stairs, then I'm in a bar where the macabre theme continues, to a soundtrack of U2 live in concert.

I ask the girl at the bar for a beer, then take a table under a pair of manacles stuffed with red carnations. The other drinkers are a student crowd in heavy metal T-shirts, which seems not inappropriate. There has to be a story behind a place like this – and there is. It's told in the framed news clippings on the exposed brickwork; but I don't understand a word, so I imagine it's the work of a mad, bone-collecting art lover with a taste for Grand Guignol. The ceiling has a skull at each corner, with a blowhole to let the demons out or the candles in.

And on every side there are dusty display cases, containing the bones of rats and rabbits, chickens – even a porpoise. All are preserved in antic poses, oblivious to the fact they're committing the ultimate in going about underdressed.

I suddenly feel like talking to Duncan. But I left my mobile at the hotel and it wouldn't work down here anyway. He emailed me the details of a date he was going on last night and I want to hear how it went. I also want to tell him I'm sitting in a cellar in Ljubljana, with whale bones and Bono wailing, waiting for a self-inflicted showdown with someone I never wanted to speak to again as long as I live. I have an unaccountable thirst on; my glass is empty in minutes. By the time I'm halfway down the second, I couldn't tell you why I changed my mind – or even what I want to say.

'Anthony! I was just passing when I saw you through the window. And since I've never had the chance to see if I've really, totally erased you from my life, I thought I'd pop in and check!'

'Anthony! Fancy seeing you here! I was wondering – are you still the nasty, manipulative, lying shit you used to be, or are you reformed?' (Like pork.) *'Thing is, I've got a crazy idea you're the reason why I'm nearly forty and incapable of having a relationship – how do you feel about that?'*

'Blimey, rabbit on the menu! Is it related to one downstairs? And talking of dead things, did you know that on the rare, undoubtedly pointless occasions I think about going to heaven, I never imagine meeting a hotter version of any decent man I ever met. Just a kinder version of you ...'

By the third pint, I'm still undecided. But it's crushingly obvious I wouldn't be here if I was really over him. Which means I'm either being very stupid and treading dangerous emotional ground, or seeking a tiny bit of his poison to act as an antidote.

(An anthony-dote?)

('Anthony – *don't!*')

I laugh at my own jokes all the way to the bar, and ask for the toilets.

'On stairs, behind the books,' says the girl, like she gets asked it every night.

On the … ?

She's right. The case of leather-bound volumes swings away from the wall, just like in the movies. Behind is a handbasin and two doors; the mad bone collector certainly had an eye for detail.

Secret passage, trap door ... Isn't this *exactly* the kind of place that a man with an evil twin would be working?

I check my watch. Five past nine.

*

At the top of the stairs the door is still shut, but it opens when I push it.

Inside it's brightly lit and the white of the tablecloths hurts my eyes. The restaurant is set for dinner but empty of customers, and HEYBOB80 was right – it's tiny. I hear someone moving around in the kitchen and I don't know whether to stand or sit. And if I sit, should I be facing him when he comes out? Or be where he won't see me, so I see him first?

And if he is in the kitchen, does that mean he's the chef? I mean, he wasn't a bad cook, but not what you would call professional ... My left hand is starting to twitch. I'm looking around for a menu to check for duck à l'orange when—

'For one?' says the balding guy in white overalls.

*

The chef is the waiter, maître d' and sommelier. And washer-upper probably, from what I can see. He's whipping about like a white whirlwind, even with only three tables taken. At first I jump every time the door opens. By the time I'm at the bottom of the very fine fondue, I don't even bother looking up.

Either this isn't the place or it's his night off. Anthony isn't here.

At other tables sit two couples. Middle-aged Americans, talking about a concert they saw last night, and a museum this afternoon. The other diners are two Slovenian women – sisters by the look – talking earnestly about something. One keeps taking calls on her mobile, which is on vibrate and makes the crumbs jump. When she's on the phone her voice switches between clipped and childlike, which suggests it's the babysitter phoning for back-up.

The wine is very reasonably priced, so I risk a glass on top of all that beer. I'm wondering whether to risk one more when the chef asks if I'd like dessert.

'I'll look at the menu,' I say.

Like wild horses would keep me from pud. I wonder if he's heard of treacle tart.

But Chef looks glum. 'We got only lemon cheesecake.' (*We?*) 'Or choc-o-late parfait with apricot sorbet ...'

I order the cheesecake and another glass of house white. The choice is limited in all courses, but the food has been good so far and you can't fault him for effort. The Americans head off after a minor set-to about paying with MasterCard. Before long, chef is sitting at their table with a coffee and a cigarette. Benson & Hedges, in a strange silver packet. He smiles at me when I catch his eye ... And I know I'm going to ask him, but I'm suddenly self-conscious. Even with a bulb blown in the candelabra light, it's bright enough to perform eye surgery in here. I can also hear every word those women are saying, and I bet they understand English ...

What the hell.

'So, do you work here on your own?'

Chef smiles. I wonder if it sounded like a chat-up line.

'Yes,' he says with a drag of his fag. 'Right now.'

'It must be hard, doing everything.'

He nods. Raises his eyes to the ceiling.

'I very tired ... I been for *two weeks*.' He stirs another sugar into his cup.

'Two weeks ... ?'

'By my own. The other guy, he leave.'

Ah.

'Was he, erm – British, by any chance?'

He nods.

The woman without the phone leans over and asks for the bill.

'Was he – was he called Anthony?'

'No.'

'Or Tony?'

'No.'

Chef takes a pad and calculator out of his pocket.

'He was James … He work here for two month and then …' He flicks a hand dismissively, sending a boulder of ash into the sugar crystals.

James. I bet he was. That's his middle name.

Above the door is a four-foot-long glass box in the shape of a coffin. Lying inside, propped up on one elbow like a bored concubine, is a skeleton in a top hat and tatty red cloak. This, according to the plaque, is Rico himself. He is looking down on us, watching proceedings with the signature fixed-grin that presumably gives the place its name.

I ask for my bill, too. Chef brings it with three little sweets in purple wrappers, like dolly-sized Quality Street.

'You are look for him?' he asks.

Dinner was ridiculously cheap. I flick through the unfamiliar currency and put it in the saucer.

'No, I … No, not really.'

After one last trip to the world beyond the bookcase, my change is waiting. I work out the tip in tolars and put the rest in my pocket.

Chef comes off the phone in the kitchen and nods politely.

'Thank you,' he says. And 'Goodnight.'

Outside, the music still booms from downstairs. By now, the bar will be packed solid and, befittingly, smoky as hell. I wish I'd brought something with sleeves; it's chillier than I expected. Then again, it is nearly midnight.

The alley slopes down in the direction of the river. Through the far opening I can see lights dancing on the water. And I'm just thinking I'll follow it round to the dragon bridge – go back to the hotel that way – when it happens.

Walking around London at night, you develop an early-warning system. On my way home from the Barrel, I make a point of being aware of anyone in a fifty-metre radius. I've pretty much got it down to a fine art. So it's a jolt, on the rare occasion I'm too blotto or preoccupied to flick the on-switch, when someone gets close without me knowing.

That's how it is tonight. There I am, halfway down the tunnel, woozy with booze and mulling over what was probably a lucky escape from my past, when the voice behind me says:

'Wotcha, Dan. I bet it's not this cold in Helsinki.'

CHAPTER THIRTY

I'm out of that tunnel in four strides. Don't look round till I am.

He emerges three paces behind me, into a pool of light under the sign with the jittering skulls. He is tall and slim, wearing a brown leather jacket. And I don't have a clue who he is, which is a relief and a head-fuck, too. Further along the street, two lads are peering into a shop window. I stand my ground, show him I'm not freaked out. But it's only because there are people around.

'Do I know you?'

He looks pale in the glow of the street lamp.

'Sorry,' he says, 'I didn't mean to startle you.'

So much for trying not to look startled.

'You didn't, it's just … Who the fuck are you?'

'I'm Simon Wolf.'

Cue the sound of a penny not dropping.

'We were chatting this afternoon – I'm Maestroman.'

My mind snaps a Polaroid of this moment: him, standing beneath the row of fluorescent white skulls, one hand fiddling with the zipper of his jacket. In the darkness behind me, someone swishes past on a bike.

'Oh. Right,' is the best I can come up with. 'Well, 'scuse me for being a slowcoach, but I assumed you were in London.'

'I know. Sorry.'

'Were you in London?'

'No. I'm staying at Hotel Lev. I'm here for—'

'Why didn't you say so?'

He shuffles awkwardly. 'Do you mind if we walk for a bit? I feel a bit conspicuous standing in a spotlight …'

We walk along the river. Him nearer the water, while I wait for an explanation.

'I'm here to do a concert. Part of the festival. When you said you were here as well, I didn't know what to say.'

'How about, "Hey, you won't believe this – I'm in Ljubljana, too." And, "Do you fancy a drink?"'

I'm getting snippy. I can hear it.

'Yeah, all right!' snaps Simon. 'It's not that simple …'

His tone says I'm near a line and I'd better not cross it.

Neither of us speaks for a minute. Then I say:

'So, what's this concert you're doing?'

'Ligeti, *Fugues and Silences*.'

He notices my nodding, brisk but clueless.

'You know it?'

'Are they like Earth, Wind & Fire?'

This gets a laugh. He has a nice laugh.

'… I've got one of their albums – must be before you joined …'

We keep walking until we reach the dragon bridge.

'We could get a drink somewhere,' I say. 'The bars are still open, this isn't London.'

'I'd like to but I'd better not. I've got the gig tomorrow and I need a decent sleep.'

Oh, right then. Well, I've had some funny encounters in my life – but this … I'm getting one straight answer whether he likes it or not.

'You were looking for me, though, weren't you? You're not going to say you were passing down a dark alley and just happened to recognise me from my photos?'

'Yeah, of course I was looking. And I did recognise you from your photos. I tried a couple of other restaurants that sounded like the one you were looking for.'

'What, more than "Rico The Happy Skeleton"?'

He smiles and looks away. 'Then I found you. Just in time … Look, this feels really strange. Can I see you tomorrow?'

'I'm leaving tomorrow—'

'Me too. What time?'

'Quarter to three.'

'Okay. Let's meet in the morning. Where are you staying?'

I find a card for the hotel in my back pocket.

He takes it. 'Oh, very organised…'

'Yeah, well – that's me for you. Rule Number One in a strange town: Always carry the hotel address in case you get lost, drunk, or the cabbie's cute and offers to shin up your drainpipe later …'

'Wise,' he nods. 'Though if the cabbie can't remember where he dropped you, you have to wonder if he'd know what to do when he got there …'

Ouch. No one likes a smart-arse.

'I'll call for you at ten, Dan.' That smile again. 'We can go and feed the ducks.'

Though in his case, I could make an exception.

CHAPTER THIRTY-ONE

I'm lying half in, half out of the duvet with the evening whirling round my head.

I've been awake for what seems like hours, mulling over the oddness of it all. In the months since we began chatting, I've formed a picture of Maestroman. All his profile says is that he's slim, dark and six foot three, so I've filled in the rest myself. Gleaming eyes, mad *Amadeus* hair; shoulders hunched in anticipation of his next thunderous chord …

I didn't get much of a look at his eyes, but I was wrong about the hair. His posture I can check tomorrow. I wouldn't say he's one of my usual types – but then he didn't invite me back for baton practice either, so …

In fact, I still don't know why he tracked me down at all, given that he has body-swerved every proposal I've ever made. At the back of my mind, I was resigned to the fact we'd probably never meet. After the initial flurry our chats have become less frequent. I thought we'd probably missed our moment.

In a hiss of brakes a dustcart pulls up three floors below; there's the familiar cacophony of bins and yelping voices with no respect for the hour. A thin edge of light is hinting at the curtains as tiredness tips me into sleep. And my final conscious thought is relief: to be ending the day preoccupied with a different man from the one it started with.

*

As I watch the lights count down from 3 to G, I realise I can't remember what he looks like. This is not unusual: it often takes a lot more than a nocturnal stroll for me to commit a face to memory.

When the lift doors open, he's in reception, smiling from the sofa. He's wearing long shorts, a linen jacket and a vest, above the arc of which three chest hairs are peeping.

'Hey, Dan. How did you sleep?'

'Not bad. Have you had breakfast?'

I was too knackered to obey my mobile's 9 a.m. summons, but the self-serve jams and giant bowls of cereal are still out in the bar.

'Yeah. Come on, I'll buy you something in the park.'

I nip in and swipe a banana from a platter that could be decorative or feng shui, turning on my heel before the servers can object.

Outside, it is sunny and mild. Simon puts on his shades: smoky wraparounds, an understated version of the style favoured by Yoko Ono and welders.

'Sorry about last night,' he says. 'You must think I'm a weirdo.'

I shrug. 'You gave me a fright, but I know you didn't mean to. Which way?'

He points towards a junction, beyond which lie iron railings and high foliage, dense as broccoli.

'I assure you, I'm not in the habit of tracking down strange men in the middle of the night ...'

'No? Don't tell me – you're only on click4dick to swap recipes.'

'Touché,' he laughs. 'What I mean is, I'm not in the habit of doing it in person. And I know we could have met before – it's me who's been dragging my feet.'

I shrug. 'I didn't think you were interested ... Happy to chat, but that's that. Plenty of guys are like that, which is fine if it's all they want.'

We come to a main road, with cars and lorries lumbering by. There's an underpass, but first we have to negotiate the cycle paths that seem to be everywhere here, slicing the pavements into strips.

'Mind out!' yells Simon, as I'm nearly swept away by a battalion of Slovenian teens on two wheels.

The concrete underpass exhibits some highly competent graffiti, including a mural of Gotham City-style skyscrapers that look nothing like Ljubljana. The artist has even integrated a rusty ventilation grille into a tower bloc, showing excellent use of perspective.

'And I *was* interested, Dan,' he says in a low voice. 'I wanted to save you.'

Oh, here we go – now he's got me back in a tunnel, he turns out to be some mad evangelist!

'From what? I don't need saving!'

'No, you turkey ... I mean, I wanted to save *meeting* you. For when it was the right time.'

'You're losing me again, Maestro.'

'Don't call me that!' His eyes are firmly on the ground. 'Please ... This is the real world.'

We come up among rose borders and primly fenced lawns. I drop my banana skin in a litter bin. This park is called Tivoli, same as the one in Copenhagen. But this one is peaceful, minus the fairground rides and the forced jollity.

Simon sighs. 'Look, I've no idea what you think of me. Beyond what I know from our chats, I don't know much about you either, but ...'

He's still studying the grey shale chippings, collecting his thoughts.

'Okay, cards on the table … I have these three imaginary in-trays. For guys I meet online. There's Would-Do, Wouldn't-Do – and Hmmm.'

This is the first overtly sexual reference he has made. Barring our one night of drunken cybersex, he's never actually admitted to using click4dick for the same reasons I do. I had him down as shy, monogamously-spoken-for, or pushing ninety. He's never invited enquiries into his private life – that's not what our chats were about. Deep down, if I did meet him and he turned out to be available and not a geriatric, I guess I hoped he'd be better than that.

Better than me.

'You see, the Would-Do tray is fairly well stacked, though any I do hook up with tend to end up in the bin soon after.' (Oh – he is a bit like me, then!) 'Whereas Wouldn't-Do is up to the ceiling. And Hmmm... Well, the Hmmm pile just kind of sits there. Daring me to do something about it.'

We stop at a utilitarian-looking fountain and sit on a bench.

'I broke up with my boyfriend a year ago. That's when I started the net thing. We'd been together seventeen years.'

'*Seventeen!*'

'Since I was twenty-one. He was the first legal lay I ever had. We moved in together two weeks later.'

An old man nods as he ambles past us, a terrier trotting at his heels.

'… When you end something like that, you just want to have fun – I did, anyway. In all the time we were together, he and I never slept around. An open relationship wasn't for us.'

Admirable. Nice to know it works for some.

'So I moved out. Got my own place, got laid. I'd never done the whole gay-scene thing, but you know what it's like on the net. After sleeping with the same man for seventeen years, it was like stumbling on Eldorado.'

I nod slowly. 'But I thought you'd need to have pics on there. To get attention.'

'I did, to begin with. Nothing saucy, but recognisably me. Then I was doing a concert in Edinburgh. Walked into the promoter's office and found him and his minions, tittering over my profile ... He's a nasty piece of work, on there all the time. He made out I'd been hounding him for sex, without realising who he was. Utter bullshit ... It wasn't a big deal at the end of the day – it's gays a-go-go in my business – even so, I didn't like it.'

I take a breath while I process this. 'On that subject – I still don't really know what you do.'

Simon smiles. 'I play piano. And compose a bit. Contemporary classical, that sort of thing.'

Two flower borders away, the old man's dog is chasing crows. Three of them fly our way and land beside the fountain. Odd-looking things: massive, with plumage smudging from black to ash, like they're wearing shawls.

'Okay. You've never been very forthcoming when I asked you.'

'I know. Sorry. You and I got chatting just after I'd taken the photos off. I avoided talking work to anyone after that. You never know who they are – or who's peeping over their shoulder.'

The fountain looks like upturned satellite dishes arranged into a pyramid. Two crows bathe in the smallest bowl while the third one looks disdainfully on.

'Gay culture's all about being *out*,' says Simon. 'Being out there. And I'm all for it, if it's what you want … But some people only feel truly accepted when they've got every facet of themselves on show to the world. I don't want that. I want to keep some of me for *me*.'

Well, I was right about one thing. He is more than your average online cruiser.

'Simon – sorry if I've got the wrong end of this but … *am I a Hmmm?*'

He turns and looks me in the eye. 'I think so.'

He has very distinctive ears. On the outermost edge of each is a tiny spur of flesh. It looks like where they were joined to the frame, before someone pressed them out and assembled them with all the other bits of the 'Thoughtful Pianist' kit.

'Do you think I could be one, too?' he asks.

I would quite like to touch them.

*

We find a stall selling hot dogs. He buys two and I eat them both, but save the second roll for the ducks.

I'm feeding my half to a pair of ornamental beauties, with scary phosphorescent eyes like the Hound of the Baskervilles.

'So why did you come looking for me here – after all this time?'

He flicks crumbs into the path of a charging moorhen.

'I nearly did it a month ago. I had a gig at the Festival Hall and I was going to invite you along, but we were never online at the same time … God – look at his feet!'

The moorhen has clambered fearlessly onto the path. It has extraordinary, blue-peapod toes.

'I don't go in for mystical stuff. But when you said you were here yesterday, I thought: Okay – it's a sign.' Simon winks. 'Then when I saw you dunking your meatballs into your little fondue ...'

'You what?'

He laughs. 'I lied. I actually found your restaurant straight away. Saw you through the window, but I couldn't just walk in and pull up a chair, could I? So I was circling the block till you came out – you took so bloody long, I thought you were waiting for someone ...'

If I didn't know better, I'd swear that duck just pursed its beak.

'I nearly bottled out. You'd think I was mad, creeping up on you a thousand miles from home in a restaurant full of skeletons.'

I laugh too, as the ducks squabble over the last bit of bread. 'Yeah, well. We all do crazy things sometimes.'

'*Shit!*'

Simon jumps off the bench.

'Quarter to twelve. I've got to get back!'

Which reminds me ...

'So are you really flying back to London after the concert? I didn't think they flew at night.'

'Eh? Oh, no ... When I said I was leaving today, I meant leaving Ljubljana. My concert's fifty miles away. In a church. At a place called Bled.' He touches my hand. 'Will you come?'

'I can't!' My voice shoots up like he dropped an ice cube down my neck. 'I mean, I'd love to, but I've got a train to catch ... I never told you, but I'm meant to be in Italy. I shouldn't be here at all ...'

CHAPTER THIRTY-TWO

There's a song by Liza Minnelli. About a girl who goes halfway round the world and meets a guy who turns out to be her next-door neighbour.

Simon Wolf lives in Abercrombie Road, Clapham, London SW4. That's three streets from my flat. Simon also knows that Liza Minnelli song, and we hum it through miles and miles of deepest Slovenia. Our driver does not know the Liza Minnelli song. Or if he does, he's keeping it quiet, possibly to avoid competing with my perfect pitch.

We stop at a garage with a shop that sells T-shirts, though not underwear or socks. It also sells CDs of Slovenian accordion polkas, one of which the driver buys. He plays it all the way to Bled.

Simon says accordion polkas are an important part of Slovenian heritage. I say my Gary Numan bootlegs are an important part of *my* heritage, but I wouldn't play them in the car when someone else is paying. The driver doesn't say anything.

Simon doesn't laugh when I mention Gary Numan. He is becoming more of a Hmmm all the time.

*

'*Simon, hi!* You made it!'

This is Nerisa, Simon's publisher. She has come over from London and is helping to organise the festival. She has called him twice in the last five miles, and as we pull up beside the lake she is there to meet us. We're late, apparently.

'Dave and Mike are already at the church. I've spoken to the tuner and told him to hang on till you get there, okay?'

'Thanks, Nerisa. This is Dan.'

'Dan, hi! Let me get someone to run your bags up to the hotel. I'm not sure if you guys'll have time to freshen up – we'd better get you to the church ... on time! Ha-ha!'

The lake is bounded on three sides by high cliffs thatched with firs. It is utterly tranquil and unspoilt, to the extent that a green-and-yellow festival banner tied to a gate feels like vandalism. Across the road, a scattering of buildings with red tiled roofs constitute the village, though from the name I'd expected something a bit more Transylvanian. One building looks like it might be a hotel, but I can't see anything with a spire.

'Where's this church, then?'

Simon puts his hands on my shoulders. Then he swings me round to face the lake.

'There.'

*

Three boats are ahead of us as we skim across the water. At the stern of each is a hefty bloke leaning forward on one foot. He churns away at the water with a pair of oars, like frog's legs.

Simon and Nerisa are going through papers, talking about agents and fees and recording contracts. This is a whole new world.

Our oarsman is whistling to himself as I pull my elbow into the shade of the canopy, feeling it start to burn. I stick my head out and look at the empty sky. Round about now, I should be having my passport inspected by Italian border guards. Or rather, having a beer on the terrazzo in Trieste. Or rather, wondering what I'm going to watch after *EastEnders*.

Funny old world, eh?

*

Our oarsman ties us up to the jetty. Then Nerisa, then I, then Simon clamber giddily onto the island. The church is at the top of a flight of crumbling steps that look like something excavated at Pompeii. There are more banners here, some with Simon's name on.

'Got to see the piano tuner,' he says. 'Come in if you want, but you might find it a bit boring.'

'Sure. I'll just have a quick look round. Do I need to buy a ticket?'

He leans over and kisses me on the cheek. 'Nerisa's got one for you. Sorted.'

It disturbs me that I can have sex at the drop of a hat, but when someone kisses me out of the blue, I don't know how to handle it. A boatload of tourists milling in the sunshine unsettles me far more than any number of grunting, anonymous men in the half-light. I'm embarrassed, but only at myself.

There's a stall selling ice cream and souvenirs. It has two different postcards of the little church, on its island in the middle of the lake. They're taken from the same spot, one in summer and one in snow. I'm drawn to the latter, for its dazzling whiteness; with its frozen surface caked in snowdrifts, and the spectral trees suspended in the breath of winter, Lake Bled looks like somewhere on another planet.

I buy a couple of cards, and a snow dome for Gina. She was all right when I called to say I was staying an extra night, though I distinctly heard her eyebrows crank up when I told her why. ('Just once!' she said. 'You could let me bask in being the femme fatale *just once* …')

But when I asked about Gareth, she was breezily evasive.

'Oh, you know. Fine.'

When I get back to her tomorrow, there'll hardly be time for a drink before we head for the airport. This has not been the trip either of us expected.

By seven o'clock, the flotilla of skiffs has ferried across an audience of about a hundred. We take our seats in the nave, and I squeeze in behind a white-haired man and woman engrossed in the information sheet we were handed at the door. A grand piano stands incongruously by the font. Behind it, a couple of blokes are poking around with cables, adjusting an arc lamp. But there's no sign of Simon.

The church is ornate and a little macabre. I'm sitting in the shadow of the Altar of St Anne, a towering monolith of mottled brown marble that looks like it was carved out of Pedigree Chum. At the top, among the gilt curlicues and inevitable cherubs, are what look like disembodied dolls' heads with painted-on lips and hair. I don't know what Simon had in that holdall of his, but I have a vision of him round the back of the pulpit, whisking on an Alice Cooper wig as Nerisa does his eyes.

The lights dim and come up again, like a grid fluctuation. The audience fall quiet, then the lights go down for good. Simon appears from stage left in a jade silk jacket and black trousers. He takes his seat at the piano, seemingly oblivious to the applause. He cranks up the stool a fraction by turning a little wheel on the side. Then, as the clapping subsides and without a hint of pre-minstrel tension, he starts to play.

I don't know much about classical music. But I know Beethoven when I'm not hearing it, and I'm not hearing it now. The music isn't structured or even melodic in the way I expect piano pieces to be. It's more like a stream of consciousness channelled through the keys, or a soundtrack for experimental dance. Some of the movements end abruptly, and at one point I mistake a pause for a finish and nearly clap. Everyone around me is rapt and seems to know the programme well. The man in front nods sagely after one particular piece, tapping his walking stick approvingly on the flags.

The second half of the concert is something for harp and cello, so the piece before the interval is Simon's finale. His fingers fly with the passion of the composition, sometimes landing with a thud that makes me wince. He's in the zone, just him and the piano, from where a cascade of tinkling shards and booming chords fill the church to the rafters. All I can think is, I hope he isn't hurting his fingers.

By the end the music is still a mystery, but from the reaction of the audience I'm on my own there. When he stands to take a bow with hands behind his back, he sees me and smiles. I'm very slightly awestruck. How must it feel to have all these people clapping just for you? Whatever he says, he doesn't look like a man who has qualms about standing in a spotlight.

Outside, I eavesdrop on anyone speaking English,

listening as they praise or appraise him. As the audience is going in for the second half, he appears from a door at the side. He's already back in his shorts and T-shirt. Two girls, probably students, stop him to chat, so I buy us both a choc ice.

'What did you think?' he asks cautiously, when the girls have gone off with their autographed info sheets.

'Yeah, it was … great. I've never heard anything like it before.'

He smiles and takes the ice cream. 'Not the most accessible stuff in the world. It takes a bit of getting used to.'

Nerisa scampers out from the porch. Arching up on tippy-toe, she kisses him on both cheeks.

'Simon – *fantastic!* The Ligeti knocked their socks off!'

'Thanks. It's tricky, but I think I nailed it.'

'You did, you did … So, shall we see you boys for dinner tonight? The restaurant in the castle is very acceptable!'

Castle?

'Maybe,' says Simon, looking at me thoughtfully. 'We'll head over there now. See how we feel …'

'What did she mean – castle?' I say, as Nerisa runs back into the church.

And for a second time, he puts his hands on my shoulders … There it is, high on a sheer rock face, on the far side of the lake. The stone walls and battlements are the colour of the cliff and look as if they grew right out of it. But the roofs are the same red tiles as the little buildings far below.

'Have you ever slept in a castle?' he asks, leaving his hands where they are.

'I don't think I have.' I say. 'But it's definitely one of those things you're meant to do before you're forty …'

'Then tonight's your lucky night. Come on, let's get the boat.'

As we make our way down the steps, I'm smiling all the way. Because I've got the perfect answer for Gina, when she berates me for leaving her alone in Trieste for an extra night.

She knows as well as anyone, I can't resist a man with come-to-Bled eyes.

CHAPTER THIRTY-THREE

'So, do I get to meet any of your friends before this party, or are you throwing me in at the deep end?'

We're having dinner in Faraday's, the closest thing to a posh restaurant within staggering distance of my flat. Today is my Big Four-O minus two days. I have been regaling Simon with stories of happy times and places; a few too many, perhaps, but that's the New Zealand chardonnay. My birthday bash is on Saturday night. Nothing flashy: just booze and nibbles and a bit of a boogie at my place.

'Well, you've met Dunc and Gina, and you'll meet Sandra tomorrow if you're around in the afternoon.' I say. 'She's dropping in on her way to an interview, to pick up some ads we did.'

'Okay – she's the one you used to work with, who's now looking for a job on her own?'

'That's the one. Seems like she's missing it more than I am – the deadlines, the creative buzz, the social bit. Says she can't remember the last time she was face-down on a pool table ...'

'You make all your friends sound as disreputable as you, Mister HornyDSW4.'

'Mmm,' I say into my soup. He's making a habit of spotting my defence mechanisms. Unsettling, but I like it.

We've done a lot of talking in the two weeks since we got back from Slovenia. Played it cool too, after a fashion. It would be easy to spend too much time together when you live ten minutes apart. Simon teaches a bit, as well as performing and composing; but like me, he's often around in the daytime ... Meeting him has made me think about my own career. I've started to wonder if I could support myself another way, without going back to the nine-to-five. And how little I could actually live on, in exchange for a life free of rush-hour tubes and office politicians.

Shelley Pembridge has been on the phone again. She reckons slimeball Gavin Horner wants to see me about a job at Warp Direct. The prospect still makes me shudder; not everyone in the world deserves a second chance.

I like Simon, a lot. A scary amount, in fact. There's a serenity about him, and a sort of fully-formedness I don't encounter that often. He knows he's good at what he does, and he knows being happy matters more than being rich. I can see that now.

Plus he's sexy; full marks in the bedroom, *and* he laughs at my jokes, even if he does query the plural. And – funny peculiar – I don't seem to twitch when he's around. Still early days of course, but we've even discussed the big stuff. I'm not talking about slipping him the B.C. key – he's got his own place, he doesn't need the key to mine. I mean coming off click4dick. And if I'm making it sound like going cold turkey, then that's about right.

'So, who's in charge of the music at your party?' he asks as we're waiting for main course.

'I don't know. Are you offering? Dunc's still got his Bon Tempi from when he was eight – I could get him to bring it over.'

'Thanks,' he says. 'I don't think you could afford me ... It's not going to be Gary Numan all night, is it?'

I take a sip of wine and shake my head; alas, none of

my friends has ever shared my allegiance to the millennium-straddling synth god.

'His music's a bit of an acquired taste, I know. Bit like the stuff you play.'

Our plates arrive: salmon for him, lamb shank for me.

He is not deterred. 'What is it you like so much about him, anyway?'

Ah, now there's a question.

'I'm not sure, really. The tunes, the riffs, the scowling … Why does anyone like anyone? I was into him when I was a kid, from when he was a big star in the early eighties. Just never stopped … It's like *Doctor Who*, I guess. Part of my childhood I never grew out of.' I spear a morsel of lamb and wait for it to go down. 'I reckon ninety-five per cent of the stuff life sends you slips through your fingers. The other five per cent sticks ... If I knew why that was, I'd be a millionaire, wouldn't I?'

This makes Simon smile.

I first saw Gary Numan at the Liverpool Empire in 1983, when I was in the teeth of my fixation. It was the *Warriors* tour, when his look was all bleached hair and black leather. I was right at the front, wedged against the stage with somebody else's studs digging in my rib cage. Gary kept us waiting forty minutes after the support act. The piped music throbbed interminably, winding us up to fever pitch until finally the lights went down. His band marched on from the wings, climbing to their places on the podiums. Drums and two synths, bass and rhythm guitar leaning on the speakers, waiting for the man. Then, to the sound of me and two thousand teenage girls squealing like guinea pigs, a hatch at the back of the stage slid up and a silhouette appeared, backlit in billowing dry ice

… Spielberg went for the same effect when the aliens came out of their saucer in *Close Encounters*. Gary did it better.

I'm reminded of that moment now, as the door to the restaurant kitchen opens. This time, it's a cloud of steam and a guy in a wine-stained shirt. But my jaw drops just the way it did that night twenty years ago.

At first I think he is going to ignore me. But he's coming over.

"Allo, Dan,' he says. 'Nice to see you here. Everything okay?'

'Yeah, the, er … the lamb's great, thanks.'

A piece drops off my fork, splashing sauce on the tablecloth. I put down my knife and hold the fork in my right hand instead.

'You working here, then? Sorry – this is Simon. Simon, this is …'

'Anthony – yeah, I'm back with my ex. He owns this place now. How are you, anyway? It's been ages.'

I keep the fork exactly where it is, because I'm pretty sure it'd miss my mouth.

'Good … Yeah, good, thanks. Actually, I heard you were working abroad …'

Anthony James Duke wipes his forehead with the back of a once-familiar hand.

'I was. Been all over. Doing a bit of fact-finding.'

'Fact-finding?'

He nods. 'We're thinking of opening a place in Europe, so we've been checking possible locations.'

Simon smiles. 'That sounds like a nice way to spend the summer.' He's looking from me to Anthony and back again.

'Funny,' I drop in casually, 'I could've sworn I saw you in Helsinki. Months ago now – April?'

'April... Could have been. We did a month round Scandinavia and the Baltic. Gawd, brass monkeys or what? You should have said hallo, Dan!'

He says it like he might mean it.

I shrug. 'You were miles away. It was near the Olympic Stadium. I recognised you by your red jacket.'

Now he's looking confused.

'Dunno what I was doing down there ... Oh, you mean the football ground?' Anthony leans in, not too close. 'Probably meeting Lars. Deals the best spliff in Helsinki!' He laughs and his forehead crinkles. More than it used to, which is nice.

'Fancy you remembering my old jacket! Anyway, you won't see it again. Juno's got it now.'

'Juno?'

'The other 'arf's dog. Big brown Lab. I came home one night, found it in her basket. Think one of them was trying to tell me something!'

We all laugh. Me at the irony, but I'm not letting on. There can't be many chocolate brown Labradors around these parts. I've seen that dog out walking dozens of times – never given her owner a second thought. Come to think of it, haven't I seen her being walked by *two* blokes ... ?

'Well,' I say, 'you'd had that jacket a long time.'

'Must have,' says Anthony. And just for a second he holds my gaze.

'Anyway – enjoy your meal. Come and see us again, yeah?'

And with that, he's gone.

Despite the shock, the circumstances and the memories, it doesn't feel so bad after all.

'He seems nice,' says Simon, sitting back from his empty plate. 'Blast from the past?'

'Years ago,' I say.

And I really, really hope he doesn't notice me twitching.

'Dan …'

'What?'

'Eat your lamb. It's getting cold.'

*

It is dark when we leave Faraday's. The road is quiet, and outside the late-night grocer's they're taking in the fruit and veg; apples, bananas, new potatoes. Baby sweetcorn, bunched up like the Sagrada Familia.

'Your place or mine?' says Simon.

The sky is clear, stars hanging high against the navy blue.

'Yours, I think …' Up ahead, I spot another familiar face. 'Have you ever noticed how the surface of the moon looks like Margaret Thatcher?'

'What are you talking about now?'

This time I grab him by the shoulders. I lift his chin with an index finger.

'There, look … Eyebrows – nose … Mouth wide open, like she's spouting one of her diatribes. I used to think it was just clouds going over, but it's not. I see it every time there's a full moon.'

Simon reaches round and squeezes the back of my neck. I think he's going to tell me I'm crazy. But he's thinking about something else.

'Interesting, running into that Anthony guy. I wouldn't have thought he was your type.'

I check his expression. To make sure he's being serious.

'How do you mean? Okay, he's put on a few pounds, but—'

'I don't mean that. It's just … Well, I didn't think you liked them that girly.'

'*Girly?*'

Anthony? Ripped, rugby-shirted, rippling sex god Anthony!

'Yeah, a bit … Come on, we're none of us Bruce Willis, are we?'

That's another thing I like about Simon. No self-delusion. He's his own man; comfortable in his own skin. All right, one or two of his wardrobe choices are a bit on the lurid side – I'd like to think they might find their way to Oxfam before too long – but he's a performer, after all. You've got to cut him some slack.

'Hey, Simon,' I say soothingly. 'Don't do yourself down.'

As we stop at the kerb I get a gentle prod in the small of my back. He leans over until his lips are touching my ear.

'I didn't mean *me*, Dan …'

From over the rooftops on the other side of the street, Maggie looks down with her dark empty eyes. Like the skeleton in the restaurant in Ljubljana she is watching us, seeing all there is to see. And for once, like Rico, she has nothing to say.

ABOUT THE AUTHOR

Chris Chalmers was born in Lancashire and lives in south-west London. He has visited forty countries, swum with marine iguanas and shared a pizza with Donnie Brasco. He has written a diary since he was thirteen years old and never missed a night.

www.chrischalmers.net

How many secrets can a family hide?

Nineteen-year-old Josh Maitland is at the end of a gap-year trip round the world when a tsunami hits the Canary Islands. His family are devastated at the loss of someone they thought would outlive them all: mother Diana, advertising executive and shatterer of glass ceilings; older siblings Rachel and Jem, each contemplating a serious relationship after years of sidestepping commitment; and stepfather Colin, no stranger to loss, who finds himself frozen out by his wife's grief.

Only with the discovery of the private blog Josh was writing for his friends does the significance of his travels become clear. It reveals secrets he knew about everyone in the family – and one about himself that will change the way they think of him forever.

> *'Once again Chris Chalmers combines sensitivity and wit in his observation of human behaviour with a cracking storyline. Unputdownable.'*
> Penny Hancock, bestselling author of *Tideline*

More praise for *Light From Other Windows*

'Chalmers can bring tears to your eyes on one page and make you laugh on the next. He deftly skewers the pretensions of contemporary urban life, and his dialogue is unfailingly sharp and witty.'
Suzi Feay, Literary Journalist

It is a powerful, thought-provoking read about modern family life that will challenge comfortable assumptions. Despite the difficult subject matter its message is life-affirming. I cannot recommend it highly enough.'
neverimitate.wordpress.com

'A wonderful examination of human nature and relationships … The timing of the writing pulled me into the lives of the Maitland family and kept me turning page after page. The use of description overflowed with similes, conjuring sparkling imagery that fitted perfectly with the tone of the novel. A completely absorbing and entertaining read.'
livemanylives.wordpress.com

'Not a thriller, grip-lit or misery lit. It's a study of family, uncertainty and grief … Chris Chalmers is a man of words that blend together and convey emotion with a raw intensity. Some moments are dripping with sadness whilst others release silent sarcasm and wry wit. The end result is a novel of substance; slow, sensual and utterly mesmerising.'
bleachouselibrary.ie

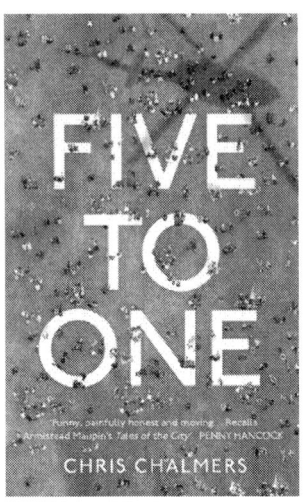

Nominated for the Polari First Book Award
Winner of the Wink Publishing Debut Novel competition

Every moment starts somewhere

A care assistant with a secret. A gardener with an eye for more than greenfly. An estate agent and an advertising man, each facing a relationship crisis. And a pilot with nowhere to land.

At twelve fifty-five on a sunny afternoon, five lives converge in a moment of terror as a helicopter crashes on Clapham Common. It's a day that will change them all forever – and for some, it will be their last.

'A funny, often painfully honest and moving story about the absurdity of modern life and the concerns that propel us. Chalmers writes with a sensitivity and wit that recalls Armistead Maupin's **Tales of the City***'*
Penny Hancock, bestselling author of *Tideline*

'A poignant study of genuine love in a big and fantastically diverse city'
BytetheBook.com

More praise for *Five To One*

'Rare to find a book that makes you laugh out loud. Brilliantly observed with cracking one-liners, Five To One *is a supremely enjoyable vignette of the lives of our times, with a serving or two of pathos that holds up a mirror to us all.'*
Webbie

'A gripping and witty novel... Chalmers succeeds with an admirable denouement.'
Otleytipped

'He writes with precision both in his lapidary (occasionally snort-inducing) prose, and his character studies of lonely Londoners and their lives, in settings as diverse as New Zealand, the Galápagos Islands and Loch Ness.'
Avidreader

'Utterly hooked from the beginning. One of the finest opening chapters I've read in a long while.'
A.B. Pearl

'Characters that are not only believable but loveable too ...the end is pure genius.'
JBC

'Enormously witty.'
JaynieR

'A thoughtful, clever, often very funny novel.'
Valerie John

'I found it hard not to read this book all in one go. The fascinating mix of characters and sense of suspense gripped me from the first chapter. Fast-paced, well-written and witty throughout.'
Mightier Than The Sword

26095645R00148

Printed in Great Britain
by Amazon